"Would you take off my tie, please?" Zach murmured huskily.

Cassidy nodded and stripped it from around his neck. "Is that better?"

"Yes, but could you unbutton my shirt?"

"Are you having trouble breathing?" she asked, concerned, as she hurried to do as he asked.

"Remember when you told me you had trouble breathing when I was very close?"

Her hands slowed on the buttons. "Yes."

"I have the same trouble," Zach confessed quietly.

"I don't understand. Are you having trouble breathing? Do you need something?"

"Yes, and yes." His voice grew thicker with every word. "You." He curled his hands around her soft upper arms. "I need you to touch me."

There was something new in his eyes, she realized, and wondered why she'd been so slow to see it. The dreaminess had become focused with desire. The twinkling had changed to fire.

"Zach—"

"There's nothing wrong with me, Cassidy, that you can't fix. I want you in the worst way and I have almost from the first moment I saw you," Zach said. "Fix me. Touch me. . . ."

WHAT ARE *LOVESWEPT* ROMANCES?

They are stories of true romance and touching emotion. We believe those two very important ingredients are constants in our highly sensual and very believable stories in the *LOVESWEPT* line. Our goal is to give you, the reader, stories of consistently high quality that may sometimes make you laugh, sometimes make you cry, but are always fresh and creative and contain many delightful surprises within their pages.

Most romance fans read an enormous number of books. Those they truly love, they keep. Others may be traded with friends and soon forgotten. We hope that each *LOVESWEPT* romance will be a treasure—a "keeper." We will always try to publish

LOVE STORIES YOU'LL NEVER FORGET
BY AUTHORS YOU'LL ALWAYS REMEMBER

The Editors

Fayrene Preston
The Lady in Red

BANTAM BOOKS
NEW YORK · TORONTO · LONDON · SYDNEY · AUCKLAND

THE LADY IN RED

A Bantam Book / October 1991

If you would be interested in receiving protective vinyl
covers for your Loveswept books, please write to this address
for information:

Loveswept
Bantam Books
P.O. Box 985
Hicksville, NY 11802

ISBN 0-553-44168-X

Published simultaneously in the United States and Canada

Bantam Books are published by Bantam Books, a division
of Bantam Doubleday Dell Publishing Group, Inc. Its trademark, consisting of the words "Bantam Books" and the
portrayal of a rooster, is Registered in U.S. Patent and
Trademark Office and in other countries. Marca Registrada.
Bantam Books, 666 Fifth Avenue, New York, New York
10103.

PRINTED IN THE UNITED STATES OF AMERICA

OPM   0 9 8 7 6 5 4 3 2 1

To Kay
Who is always so easy to get on the phone

One

"Who's the lady in red?" Zach Bennett's blue-eyed stare was riveted on the woman in the long, formfitting sheath glittering with red sequins. She stood across the room from him, shimmering like a beautiful Christmas ornament, her hair a shining ash blond, her skin a burnished gold.

Beside him, Mark Landon, the friend he had questioned, shrugged. "I'm sorry to say I've never seen her before. But she fills out that dress in all the right places, doesn't she?"

Zach didn't bother to respond. One of the most spectacular parties of the season was going on in the mansion at One River's Edge. The party was a charity event to raise money for a new children's wing for the hospital. Prominent chefs from the area had donated their services, and each chef presided over several tables, ladened with their specialties. There were people

Zach should speak to, delicacies he should sample, but he couldn't tear his gaze from the lady in red.

"By the way, it's good to see you here," Mark said. "No one expected you to be able to make it back into town by this evening."

"I was able to wind up the meetings early. Are you sure you don't know her?"

"Nope. But I may try to remedy that very soon."

"Don't bother."

Underlying Zach's soft tone was a note of hard determination that made Mark lift his eyebrows. "Sure. Whatever you say."

Zach watched as a waiter offered the woman a glass of champagne. She shook her head, but then as the young man was about to turn away, she changed her mind and took a glass from his tray. She seemed preoccupied, removed from her surroundings. Not lost exactly, Zach reflected, but certainly on a different plane than the rest of the people in the room, who were laughing, talking, and eating. There was something contained about her, something mysterious."

He enjoyed mysteries. He loved Christmas ornaments. He was enticed by ladies in red. The last was something he hadn't known about himself until this evening.

He started toward her, making his way through the crowd, nodding to some people, stopping to have a word with others. But his ultimate goal never changed, and he soon reached her.

Her back was to him. One of the sleeves of her dress had slid down, exposing the tender curve of a satiny shoulder. And the low cut of the dress allowed him to follow with his gaze her straight spine clear to her waist.

He said the first thing that came into his mind. "Red is my favorite color."

She turned so abruptly, champagne splashed over the crystal rim of the glass and onto her hand. And when she saw him, her eyes widened. Smoke gray eyes, he noticed, that seemed solemn and serious.

Gazing up at him with surprise, Cassidy Stuart pressed a napkin to the champagne droplets on the back of her hand. "Would you mind saying that again?"

He laughed softly. "I'd be delighted. Red is my favorite color."

His deep voice and soft laugh rippled across rapidly tensing nerves. *Nerves? Where had they come from?* she wondered. She had been completely calm until she had turned and seen him.

Carefully, she set the champagne glass down on a small table. "I wanted to make sure. I didn't expect someone like you." She moistened her lower lip, immediately regretting her inane understatement. But in truth, she hadn't been prepared for the blatant sexuality that emanated from the man before her. He had a face that belonged on the pages of *GQ* and a body that belonged on an athletic field. He was six feet of hard muscle, with thick brown hair and blue eyes that seemed to dance with a humor she saw no reason for. A red silk tie and handkerchief added a touch of élan to the elegance of his dark suit. All in all, he was spectacular. Why him? she asked herself.

He smiled slowly. "I didn't expect anyone like you either." His gaze traced the lift of her throat, the fullness of her cleavage, and most of all, her soft, soft mouth. She made him hungry just looking at her.

She saw the heat in his eyes. The humor. And, unexpected and surprising, she saw a dreamer in those eyes. An unfamiliar tingling swept through her body, causing her to frown. She was a professional, she reminded herself, and this was strictly business. "In this instance," she said, using her coolest tone of voice, "it doesn't matter what we did or did not expect."

"Doesn't it?"

"No."

His gaze flickered to her bare shoulder. Belatedly she thought to pull up the errant sleeve of the dress.

His eyes followed the motion. "I like your dress."

She sent a quick glance around the room to make sure no one was watching them. "It's been a lot of bother. I had to rent it, and it doesn't fit very well."

"You rented it. Really?" He paused for the space of several heartbeats, considering the unusual information. Most of the women he knew ordered their dresses from New York designers.

She spared him a brief glance before resuming her scan of the room. "You're sadly mistaken if you think I have anything like this in my closet. What's more, after paying the rental fee for the dress, I had the devil of a time coming up with the one hundred and fifty dollar price for the ticket to get in here tonight. I hope it's worth it."

"Worth it?" He shifted his stance, unconsciously balancing his weight as a fighter might. "What exactly are you expecting?"

She noticed a couple watching them. To alleviate any suspicion, she quickly smiled up at him and reached out to touch his tie. "You know very well. And if anyone approaches us, we're old friends. Okay? Don't try to get too specific with the details. Just say we're old friends and leave it at that."

She was odd, he thought, but definitely intriguing. Maybe it would help matters if he introduced himself. "Okay, then, since we're going to be old friends, I'm—"

"Have a meatball."

Cassidy blinked. A woman had interrupted him by thrusting a silver platter of hors d'oeuvre–size meatballs in between them. She was one of those women of indeterminate age, with brassy gold hair fixed in an elaborate bouffant style, and she was wearing a body leotard overlaid with yards of translucent chiffon.

"The meatballs are safe," the woman said. "I made them myself." In a conspiratorial manner, she stepped closer and lowered her lids, revealing rhinestone-lined false lashes. "Whatever you do, stay away from those little mushroom things on the toast triangles with the mystery stuffing. That chef must have studied cooking at the

United States Institute for Car Care. They're pure poison."

Fascinated more by the woman than by what she was offering, Cassidy shook her head in refusal.

But Zach popped a meatball into his mouth. "Wonderful," he said with sincere appreciation. The woman batted her false eyelashes at him and flounced away. Delicately licking his fingertips, he smiled at Cassidy. "You should have tried one."

She caught herself staring at his mouth and suddenly felt like screaming. "Look, the sooner we get this over, the better. Do you know the layout of this house?"

"Uh . . ." Caught off guard by her question, he took a minute to think. His eyes fastened on one of several works of modern art hanging on a wall covered in taupe suede. Other walls held specially built shelves that were filled with displays of antique toys. The room was layered with vibrantly healthy plants and comfortable couches and chairs. He saw nothing out of the ordinary. Except her. "Yes, I guess I'm fairly familiar with it."

"Good," she said with real relief. "Then do you know a place we can go to be alone?"

"You want to be alone with me?" he asked carefully. Until this moment, he had seen himself as the aggressor in this game of flirtation.

"You don't think we're going to do it *here*, do you?" Impatience laced her tone. She had never seen blue eyes that twinkled quite as much as his did and in such a sexy way. But, she reminded herself, his eyes were very much beside the point. She had to get on with the business at hand.

"No, I guess not," he said thoughtfully, quickly reassessing the situation.

"And by the way, there will be *no* negotiating regarding price. All right?"

He nodded. "All right." He loved games, but he obviously had no idea what game she was playing *or* the rules she was playing by. His interest soared. No one had known he would be returning tonight, or he might think she was some kind of joke his friends had set up. But he supposed she could still be a high-class call girl who had somehow slipped through the security system. He took a moment to mull over that idea and decided he didn't like it at all. Whatever she was doing here, though, nothing changed the fact that he was still drawn to her, more in fact, with every passing moment. He had never paid for sex, but she tempted him. . . .

She frowned at his hesitancy. "You've never done this before, have you?"

The last time someone had accused him of being inexperienced, he had been fifteen, he thought wryly. "I've done everything I've ever wanted."

It was her turn to hesitate as she wondered why his statement sounded like a threat. "Are you absolutely certain red is your favorite color?"

His gaze swept over her red-sequin—covered breasts. "I'm crazy about it, believe me."

She sighed heavily. "Let me tell you something. I went to a lot of trouble to be here tonight, so this had better be good."

He wanted to laugh. He grinned instead. "I'll do what I can to make sure you aren't disappointed."

Behind the humor and the dreaminess, his eyes held a glint that made her slightly uneasy, even though she knew this encounter could be very important to her. She tucked her arm in his. "Okay, then, lead the way. And try not to act self-conscious. I don't want to draw any unnecessary attention to us."

"I'll do my best," he assured her solemnly.

In the corner of the room, a face that wore a miserable expression peered between the fronds of a palm tree and watched Zach Bennett walk away with the lady in red.

"A *bedroom*," she exclaimed minutes later, gazing around the large room, the suddenly worsening state of her nerves making her extra critical. "What are we doing in a bedroom—and the *master* bedroom, at that?"

His gaze was fixed steadily on her. "I thought it would be appropriate."

"A medium-size closet would have been just as appropriate," she said disparagingly, eyeing the electric train track that ran from under the big black iron bed to around the walls of the room.

"I'm game if you are."

She glanced back at him, then away again. This meeting was not going as she had planned. Being with this man in a room containing a bed rattled her. The bed seemed enormous, covered by a thick, plush burgundy comforter made of finger-deep corduroy. And as big as the bed was, *he* seemed even bigger, filling the room with a sexual presence that stifled her breathing. Her gaze stopped at the stuffed animals lined comfortably along the pillows. There was a giraffe, a hippopotamus, a kangaroo, and a lion, each looking amazingly cuddly. The sight made her even more agitated.

"Can you imagine a grown man like Zach Bennett, who is head of a major company, keeping a menagerie of stuffed animals like that on his bed?"

He took a deep breath. "Zach Bennett?"

"Yes, and to top it off they're *weird* stuffed animals. Whoever heard of a cuddly hippopotamus or a snuggly giraffe?"

"You think hippopotamuses are weird?"

"The real point," she said in exasperation, "is what kind of man has stuffed animals on his bed?"

This was getting more interesting by the minute, he thought. "What's wrong with stuffed animals?" He strolled over to the bed and picked up the small, golden lion. "Do you have something against them?" he asked, idly combing his fingers through the lion's mane.

It was the first time she had noticed his hands. He had big hands with long, tapered fingers and well-manicured nails. And his touch appeared gentle on the lion, unnervingly so. "No, of course not, it's simply that this house is *packed* with toys."

"You sound indignant. Zach Bennett does own a toy company, you know."

"And the reason he does is pretty obvious, isn't it? He's never grown up."

He replaced the lion on the bed and strolled back to her side. "That's a pretty interesting thing to say considering you don't know the man." He paused. "You don't, do you?"

"No, and I don't want to either. Look, let's just get on with it, okay?" She needed to get out of this room and away from this man. Her nerves had taken all they could.

"Okay," he said slowly, "what do you have in mind?"

"That we stop wasting time, and you show me what you've got."

"Excuse me?"

She made an impatient gesture with her hand. "Just give it to me, okay?"

His eyes narrowed slightly. "Whatever you say, but I think I'd like it better if you came and got it."

The peach tone of her skin darkened with a flush. "What's wrong with you? Do you think this is some kind of game?"

"I'm not sure," he said, "but you're incredibly lovely, and if this isn't a game, I think it's time we find out exactly what it is." In one quick, smooth move, he reached for her, pulled her against him, and brought his lips down on hers.

As soon as his mouth touched hers, alarm bells went off in her head, and simultaneously heat flooded every part of her body. Kissing a strange man in a strange bedroom in a strange house wasn't a smart move. That much was simple. What wasn't simple was what to do about the heat. It was pervasive, debilitating, addictive. It stole her initiative and made her want to wait and see what happened next.

The penetration of his tongue was deep and shockingly exciting. He was exciting, and he made her forget the purpose for her being here. Almost.

With a gasp, she twisted away from him, instinctively crossing her arms over her breasts. "I don't know what you think you're doing, but kissing wasn't part of this deal."

His heart was pounding, his lower body was aching. He wanted, needed, to pull her back into his arms and continue with the exploration of her mouth, and even further. Instead, with effort, he slipped his hands into his pockets and looked steadily at her. "Suppose you tell me what *was* part of this deal."

"You—" She went abruptly silent as a fearsome cold trickled down her spine.

"You didn't bring me up here for sex, did you?" he asked huskily.

"*Sex!*"

The look of outrage on her face was his answer. He couldn't remember the last time he had been so entertained, and that was saying a lot since he was entertained all the time.

The sleeve of her dress had once again fallen. He stroked a finger across the bare slope of her shoulder. "Suppose we start at the beginning, and you tell me why you brought me up here."

"I—" Her throat closed around the word, making it temporarily impossible for her to speak.

"Rather wait until later for that one? Okay, then, we'll start with something easy, like your name."

Watching him carefully, she tugged up her sleeve, sliding it back over her shoulder, almost as if its scant covering would offer her some kind of protection from him. "You don't know my name?" she whispered.

"And how would I know it?"

What could have gone wrong? she asked herself, glancing around the room as if she might find her answers in it. Her gaze lit on the stuffed lion, and she remembered his fingers combing its mane. The truth hit her; her eyes widened. "Good heavens," she exclaimed, "you're Zach Bennett!"

"Yes."

"Good heavens. And this is *your* bedroom."

"Yes."

"Good heavens," she said once again. "You weren't supposed to be here. You were supposed to be lending your house for this charity event, but you weren't to attend."

"That's funny. Not one single person told me I couldn't come to the party."

"No, no, of course not." She put a hand to her head. "Good Lord," she said, using a variation on her theme. Something had gone *very* wrong. She made a great effort to collect her wits. "I think I'd better go."

"Now why would you want to do that?" He moved to block her, putting himself between her and the door. "We were just getting to know each other. For instance, we've only begun to explore why you don't like stuffed animals."

"You're being ridiculous."

"*You're* the one who doesn't like stuffed animals," he pointed out gently, the twinkling of his eyes making their blue color deeper.

She shook her head. "It's obvious there's been a mistake."

"I guess it depends on how you look at it. From my point of view, everything is going remarkably well. You're wearing my favorite color, you asked to be alone with me, you came willingly to my bedroom, you gave me a red-hot kiss—"

"Will you stop it?"

"No, I don't think I will. At least, not until I get some answers. If you didn't bring me up here for sex, what did you bring me up here for?"

She balled her fists at her sides in frustration. "Despite the fact that you still play with toys, Mr. Bennett, it's got to be obvious I mistook you for someone else. Now please get out of my way."

He didn't move. "So if I have this whole thing right, and you'll have to excuse me if I don't, because after all, as you said, I *do* still play with toys, you were supposed to meet someone else. And you expected that person to give you something, but it didn't involve sex."

"That's right," she said, edging around him.

Once more he stepped in front of her. "What?"

"What?" she repeated blankly.

"What was this mysterious person supposed to give you?"

"Look, Mr. Bennett—"

"Zach."

"Whatever it was, it was between me and the person I was supposed to meet," she snapped.

He skimmed his hand lightly along the slope of her shoulder, knocking the sleeve off. "Someone you don't know. Someone you rented a red dress for. Someone who also likes red."

"Good-bye, Mr. Bennett."

"Zach, remember?"

She exhaled heavily. "Why don't you just give up and allow me to leave?"

"Chalk it up to a naturally curious personality. Plus, I'm wild about the way you kiss. Now, if you're not going to tell me about the other person who likes red, I suggest you forget him and concentrate on me. And you can start by giving me another kiss."

The amazing thing was she really thought about it. Memories of his kiss seeped through her mind and body, creating cracks in her resolve. She straightened. "If you don't get out of my way and let me go, I'll start screaming."

"Good," he said, closing the gap between them and taking her into his arms. "I'd love to hear you scream."

He kissed her, pressuring her lips open with his, delving his tongue deep into her mouth in an effort to take and taste as much of her as possible. She aroused many emotions in him, but the strongest at this moment was desire. He tightened his hold on her, fitting her curves into him.

She was beguilingly sensual, she responded to him like an alluring seductress. She was an exciting mystery. And he knew he was going to have to let her go.

But not yet. First he had to feel her.

The other sleeve had slipped off her shoulder, making it easy for him to slide his hand inside the low neckline of the dress and cup one breast. They hadn't even met, at any rate, not in the usual, conventional manner. It was too soon for this sort of intimacy, but he was unable to stop himself. He could do nothing to make her stay. The least he could do was make her remember him until he saw her again.

He caressed her, taking her fully into his hand and kneading the full, sweet softness. She gasped, and the sound shot heat straight to his groin. Her skin was hot to his touch, and her stiffened nipple teased his palm. He wanted desperately to pull her down to the bed with him and draw that nipple into his mouth while he discovered more of her. And only the hopeful knowledge that he would do just that in the not too distant future gave him the fortitude to slowly release her.

Cassidy was shocked by the cessation of feelings. She had been caught up in the fire of the kiss, *too* caught up, she realized with an abrupt pang. *What could she have been thinking of?*

"Do you still want to leave?" he asked softly.

She looked at his lips, still able to taste them. She looked at his eyes and saw the twinkle. "Yes. Very much."

"Then I'll walk you down."

"All right," she murmured, experiencing the unfamiliar feeling of floating on a cloud. Her skin still burned where he had touched her. Not since her disastrous affair in her college days had she been involved in such intimacy. But with Zach, she had had no choice. He had put his hands on her and her will had fled.

Suddenly reality brought her up short. "I mean, *no*. You shouldn't walk me down. People will talk."

"Really?" he asked with mild interest, lifting her sleeves back onto her shoulders. "What will they say?"

"There's no telling. They'll think we've been . . . having sex."

"No, they won't."

The utter confidence in his tone made her head snap up. "Why not?"

"Because we haven't been up here long enough. Everyone knows that when I make love, I make love for hours."

Her mouth fell open at his outrageous statement. He smiled. Strange, she thought, how before tonight she hadn't known how dangerous a combination humor and dreams could be in a man's eyes.

Minutes later, Zach was watching her walk out his front door. But even after she had disappeared, she remained vividly in his mind, shimmering in her red dress. He'd have to change one thing about her. Her gray eyes had been too serious, too guarded.

He signaled a waiter and whispered a brief instruction. The young man put down the tray he had been carrying and left.

The lady in the leotard sidled up to him with more hors d'oeuvres. "The chef in the funny hat is pushing miniature egg plants stuffed with partridge sausage. One bite and you'll die for sure. Have my shrimp quiche instead. You look as if you could do with some protein."

He took a tiny quiche without even glancing at the woman.

Two

Bobby Stuart bounded into the kitchen. "I don't want any breakfast, Cass." He reached his long arm across the table and scooped up a glass of orange juice.

Cassidy pointed the knife she was using to butter toast at her six-foot-tall, sixteen-year-old brother. "Sit. Eat."

"But basketball practice—"

"Doesn't start for thirty minutes. That gives you fifteen minutes to eat. You'll never get your face on the front or back of a cereal box by skipping breakfast. Sit."

He slid his lanky frame onto a chair. "I'll eat, but not because I want my face on a cereal box. I'm going for the tennis shoe commercials." He grinned. "Can't you see me on TV, selling away?"

"Uh-uh. Eat your oatmeal, Bobby, and tell me about your trigonometry test yesterday."

"No prob'," he said, dumping two spoonfuls of

sugar into the bowl, then adding milk. "I aced it."

"Good. What about English?"

"I'm thinking about making it my second language."

She plopped a plate of toast down in front of him. "Not funny."

He grinned again. "You're way too serious, sis. A basketball player of my caliber shouldn't have to worry about whether to use *lay* or *lie*. When I become an NBA player, all I'll have to worry about is fighting off the girls and signing my name to those checks I'm going to be writing. What do you want, Cass? A Jag or a Mercedes?"

Smiling, she reached out and ruffled his hair. "I want a college education for you, my love. And to get into a good school, you're going to have to know whether to use *lay* or *lie*, not to mention *affect* or *effect*."

He ate the last spoonful of oatmeal, gulped down the rest of the orange juice, and pushed back from the table. "I'll work on it between slam dunks."

"I'm going to slam dunk you—"

With two pieces of toast in one hand, he leaned down and planted a kiss on her forehead, effectively stopping her threat. "Don't worry, I'll get into a good school. It's in the bag. Gotta go now." He grabbed up his books and an apple and bolted out the door.

"See you tonight," she called after him, shaking her head and grinning. He knew how to get around her, there was no doubt about it. But he was a good kid, and she loved him with all her heart. She had raised him by herself since he was eight years old, and she had never begrudged him a moment of the time.

In an indirect way, Bobby was responsible for her being at Zach Bennett's house the previous night. The more good, solid stories she could get for the newspaper where she worked, the more promotions she would earn and the higher her salary would go. And she was going to need a lot of money in the next few years. She didn't want Bobby to have to work his way through college as she had had to do. Sometimes she thought she was more ambitious for Bobby than she was for herself. But he had a real genius for math, and engineering fascinated him. He would be a *great* engineer, she thought with pride.

With a glance at the clock, she began clearing the table and rinsing the dishes. Her expression clouded as she worked. Meeting Zach Bennett had definitely not been on the agenda the night before. But once she had, she had compounded her error by kissing him and practically melting in his arms. "Stupid, stupid," she muttered, hitting the faucet with more force than necessary to turn it off. It had been a long time since she had been kissed by a man, and she had never, ever even imagined herself being so bowled over.

It wasn't like her to let herself go as she had with him. Normally she was a calm, serious, responsible young woman, and she was very proud of that fact. But with Zach she had behaved terribly, and she had no excuse. None. She had fouled up the meeting with a man whose information might be able to help her career, and she had almost succumbed to a man who was known to love to play. She *never* played.

Great night's work, she told herself sarcastically.

She put the last dish into the dishwasher and reached for the sponge. There was nothing left for her to do but put the whole episode out of her mind, she reflected, wiping the counter with an energy that threatened to take off the finish. She also had to keep her fingers crossed and hope her informant would contact her again.

His voice had been deep, like Zach's. But now that she considered the matter, the man on the other end of the line had sounded scared, almost panicky. Zach was the most confident man she had ever met.

The image of Zach filled her mind. Damn the man and his twinkling blue eyes! She tossed the sponge into the sink and went to get ready for work.

Zach pushed his favorite toy bulldozer along his desk, scooping aside pencils and paper clips as he went.

Janet McCloskey, a brunette with shapely legs, sat in front of his desk, not at all perturbed by the unorthodox manner in which her boss was conducting this meeting. She had worked with Zach for five years and knew he was a dreamer and that playing helped him work out problems. They were meeting about the new video game Bennett Toys planned to launch in the following year.

"Part One, The Quest, of the game is just about finished," Janet said. "Another few days should do it. Wait until you see the graphics. They're great." She sneezed and with a mild oath reached for a tissue.

"The Battle will be finished at about the same time," Will Frazier said. He was an intense young man who lived computers, and he had told Zach when he had applied for the job that working in the video division of Bennett Toys would be his idea of heaven. "The graphics are extraordinary, but I think I'm most proud of the sound."

Zach switched his attention to his lime green Hot Wheels Beatnik Bandit and drove it along the path he had cleared with the bulldozer. "Did you all know that pound for pound, inch for inch, Hot Wheels are the fastest cars in the world?"

"Yes, Zach, we knew that." Brad Monroe might be the newest employee of Bennett Toys, but he already had heard Zach expound on the wonders of Hot Wheels a number of times. He also knew Zach wasn't missing a word of what they were saying. He drew a handkerchief out of the pocket of his designer suit and blew his nose. "Whenever we figure out who gave us these damned colds, I say we lynch them. Practically everyone in the building has it except you, Zach."

Mitchell Compton, an older man complete with a large family and grandchildren, and the fourth supervisor of the video group, remained silent, sipping a cup of hot tea, and occasionally muffling a cough with his hand.

"I can't wait until we can put all four parts of the game together," Will said. "It's going to blow the competition out of the water."

Zach drove the Beatnik Bandit toward a folded piece of paper, stopped a foot away, backed it up, then took it to the edge of the paper.

"We still haven't come up with a name for Part Three, the romance part," Janet said. "It might turn the kids off if we leave it with the title The Romance."

Mitchell Compton spoke up. "I agree. My grandsons, for instance, would hate it."

Zach circled the Hot Wheels around the folded piece of paper. "We'll call it The Rescue."

"That sounds good," Janet said, then had to wait a moment while she sneezed. Holding a tissue to her nose, she went on. "It may be the romance of the game, but the hero does spend the entire time rescuing the maiden."

The other three supervisors nodded.

"Now all we need is a name for the game," Will said.

Zach drove the lime green car over the folded paper. "It's The Game."

Will snapped his ball-point pen open and shut, then coughed. "Right. That's what I said. We need a name for the game. Something catchy. Anyone have any cough drops?" Three boxes were extended toward him. He chose one and helped himself.

Zach's mouth formed the sounds *vroom, vroom*, as he drove the car off the paper.

Janet passed the tissue box around.

"I kind of like Stratospheric something," Brad said, taking a tissue and a cough drop for himself. "Maybe Stratospheric Four, for the four parts of the game, and stratospheric for . . . I don't know . . ." His words trailed away, and he glanced absently at his gold watch.

Zach at last looked up at the four people in his office. "It's The Game. I'm going to call it The Game."

There was silence in the office for a full minute. Then everyone started talking at once.

"I like it."

"It's so simple, so intriguing."

"The kids are going to love it."

"Great idea, Zach."

"Thanks." He glanced back at the Beatnik Bandit and the piece of paper. "Is there anything else? Any problems? Anything I should know?"

A chorus of *no*'s answered him.

"Good, then see you later."

He scarcely noticed when they left his office. The woman, Cassidy Stuart, was on his mind. He rolled the little car out of the way and unfolded the piece of paper with her name and address on it. And he smiled.

The telephone on Cassidy's desk in the newsroom rang. "Cassidy Stuart," she answered automatically, her mind on the words of her latest article displayed on her word processor.

"You screwed up last night."

She froze. It was the same deep voice she had heard once before. "I know, and I'm sorry. But when Zach Bennett came up and said what we had agreed upon as my way of identifying you, I naturally assumed it was you."

"I damned near had a heart attack when I saw you two together."

"Well where were you? I had been standing there quite a while."

"I told you, I had other responsibilities at the party. It took some doing to get a break."

"Okay, okay, when can we meet? You're still willing to give me the information, aren't you?"

There was a pause. "Yeah, I guess so, except lady, there better not be any screw-ups this time. My nerves can take only so much."

Hers too, she thought ruefully. "Don't worry. Where do you want to meet, and when?"

"Tonight, seven-thirty. The park. Go in the east entrance, walk to the seventh park bench on the left, and sit down. Got it?"

"Yes," she said, scribbling the instructions on a notepad. "Do we need a code phrase?"

"No. I know what you look like now, and hopefully not too many people will approach you and hand you an envelope containing a transcript of a telephone conversation."

Her lips twitched. "Right. What are the odds?"

"Seven-thirty," he said and hung up.

A little after seven that evening, Zach pulled his car to a stop across the street from Cassidy's house. He was just in time to see her drive away in the opposite direction. With a curse, he made a U-turn and headed after her. He had hoped to break away from work much earlier, but Brad hadn't exaggerated when he had said practically everyone in the company was sick. Besides having to endure resentful comments about his disgustingly healthy immune system, Zach also had to be present to put out fires.

A light turned red, and he watched in frustration as Cassidy's taillights disappeared down the street. But, he reassured himself, the traffic wasn't heavy tonight, and he'd be able to catch up to her soon.

She had been alone. He smiled with satisfaction, reflecting that she was probably going out to dinner or a movie. Wherever she was going, he planned to be there too. He had gone to a lot of trouble to find out her address, and he didn't intend to let her get away from him tonight.

Ten minutes later, he was worried as he looked for her car. Then he saw it, parallel to the street by the entrance to the park, sitting empty.

He frowned as he slowed down and pulled his car to the curb. The park was an odd place for a woman alone to be going at night. His fertile imagination took a leap. Was she meeting the man she had been looking for last night? His mouth thinned. He had no idea what she was up to. He almost didn't care, finding only what concerned the two of them important. But it seemed very plain to him that he would have to clear this mystery out of the way so he could get down to having a relationship with her.

She had mistaken him for someone else, he had misunderstood the things she had said, and he had found the whole encounter vastly amusing. But he was also aware that she hadn't found it the least bit funny. What was the man to have given her? It was obviously something important to her. Why? Could she be in some kind of trouble?

Unfortunately, whatever the answers were, he knew they weren't going to come easily.

He was intuitive enough to realize he couldn't use bulldozer methods with Cassidy. With her he couldn't plow straight ahead as he had today with his toy bulldozer, pushing all obstacles out of the way until he had found out what he wanted to know. Instead, he would have to circle her, picking up what he could on his own until she chose to give him more.

One way or the other, though, he would solve the puzzle. And this time he had a feeling the prize would be infinitely sweeter than any he had ever won before.

Cassidy found the seventh bench on the left and sat down. She glanced around her nervously. She hadn't seen another person since she had entered the park. She rubbed a clammy hand down her jeans. The nearest light pole was two benches down, which left her bench in shadows.

Where *was* he? *Who* was he?

He had called her out of the blue a couple of days before and told her that he had read an investigative article she had done several months before on kickbacks a city councilman had received. The article had been her first and so far only important investigative piece, with her first and so far only by-line, and she was extremely proud of it. The city councilman was now awaiting trial. The caller had gone on to ask her a few questions, as if to assure himself he could trust her, then he had told her about overhearing a telephone conversation at Bennett Toys. Someone there was planning to steal the design for Bennett's latest video game and sell it to a foreign buyer for ten million dollars. When they met, he had said, he would give her an almost verbatim transcript of the call and relate the circumstances under which he had heard it.

She had immediately leaped at the opportunity. Industrial espionage was big business these days, and though a video game wasn't exactly a state secret, the game *was* worth millions to someone. Maybe even more importantly, Bennett Toys was a local company employing over a thousand people. Anything that affected the livelihood of so many was bound to be a big story. Her editor had been skeptical, but in the end had said that if she could finish the assignments she already had, she could have a week to track down the story.

If he would just show up!

"Red really is my favorite color, you know. It wasn't a line."

She spun around on the bench so fast, she had to grab its back to steady herself. *"Zach!"*

Looking devastatingly attractive in black slacks and a cream-colored knit shirt, he dropped down onto the bench beside her and lightly brushed a finger over the cotton of her T-shirt. "Pretty."

Bewildered she looked down and almost groaned. When she had changed out of her work clothes into her jeans this evening, she had grabbed a T-shirt at random. The T-shirt was red. She cast a quick glance around, hoping her contact hadn't arrived yet and wouldn't see Zach. "What are you doing here?"

"Following you."

"You're *what*?"

"I saw you leaving your house, I wanted to see you, so I followed you and here I am." He shrugged, as if he had explained everything, but he understood her problem. He was interfering with her plans. But he had a problem too. He couldn't leave her alone in a park at night to meet a man she obviously didn't know. The set up had the potential to be very dangerous, and he wouldn't leave any woman alone under the circumstances, much less Cassidy. She was not only a puzzle he wanted to solve, she was a woman he wanted to have.

"You're got to leave. Now!"

He shook his head. "I don't think so."

"Why not?" Anxiety made her voice higher than usual.

He stretched his long legs out in front of him, settling himself comfortably. "Because I want to see you, and this is where you are. What's more, you're as nervous as a cat. It makes me eager to stick around and find out what or who has affected your nerves so badly."

How could a man be so laid back, she wondered, and at the same time emit so much magnetic energy? "Then look no further, Zach, because it's *you*. And in my defense, most women would be nervous if they had a man following them."

"Why? My intentions might have to go a ways before they're one hundred percent honorable, but basically I only want to spend some more time with you, get to know you. You can't be afraid of me. You were a guest in my home last night."

"I wasn't a guest," she said through gritted teeth. "I paid for the privilege."

"Come back with me now, and I'll let you in free."

"*No*. And that's my final answer. Now will you please leave before you spoil everything?"

He smiled. "So you are waiting for the other man who likes red. I thought you might be when I saw that you'd come into the park. I'm looking forward to meeting him."

It was getting worse and worse, she thought with despair. "You can't meet him."

"Why? We both like red. We probably have a lot of other things in common too."

"*Zach!*"

"Yes, Cassidy?"

"You know my name?" she asked, shocked. He also knew where she lived, she realized suddenly, because he had said that he had seen her leaving her house.

"Last night I sent a waiter after you to copy down your license plate number for me, then used a contact I have down at the Department of Motor Vehicles to trace it."

She groaned. "What's it going to take to get you out of this park?"

"For you to come with me."

"No."

"Fine, then we'll stay here, and you can tell me what this is all about."

"No."

"Okay. I'm flexible. We'll neck. We were very good at it last night. Remember?" He reached over and placed his finger on her bottom lip.

God must have shorted ten men in the charm department when He made Zach, she thought, feeling herself quiver at his touch. "What time is it?"

He raised his arm and looked at his watch. "Seven forty-five."

"Good heavens, Zach, is that really a Mickey Mouse watch?"

"I've had it ever since I was a boy," he said, holding it closer to her so that she could see it better. "Do you like it?"

Her brain couldn't even begin to cope with the idea of a Mickey Mouse watch on a man who could scorch her insides with a mere kiss, so she switched her thoughts to something she could cope with—the man she was supposed to meet here. In all likelihood, he had probably already shown up, taken one look at Zach, and run. Damn. Damn. Damn. She stood.

"Are we leaving?" Zach asked, also standing.

Without answering, she began walking toward the park exit.

He fell into step beside her. "Where are we going?"

"*I'm* going home."

"Great," he said with genuine enthusiasm. "I've seen the outside of your house, I'd like to see the inside."

She stopped and looked up at him. They were standing beneath a light, making it easy for her to see the hard angle of his jaw, a remarkable contrast to the dreaminess of his eyes. "No."

He sighed. She was going to take some convincing. "Cassidy—" he began.

"Just listen to me. I'm sure you're a very nice man, but I have no wish to become involved with you or with anyone. I admit that last night I overreacted somewhat to your kiss, but—"

"Overreacted?"

"But," she said, going on determinedly, "that was because you caught me off guard, and—"

"Cassidy, Cassidy . . ." His tone was gentle as he laid his hand on her cheek.

She tensed, viewing the renewed twinkling of his eyes as extremely ominous.

"I'm sorry," he said. "I wish I could tell you that if you continue with your explanation, it will make me go home alone, but I can't. Because you see, not only am I wildly attracted to you, I can't help but feel that whatever you're involved in has something to do with me. Maybe it's because I keep showing up instead of the other man. Maybe it's because I don't like the idea of you meeting a stranger in a deserted place at night. Or maybe it's just because I really do like the color red, especially on you. But whatever the reason, I want another opportunity for you to overreact to my kisses."

His touch on her face warmed her skin. The huskiness of his tone stirred something in her. But, she forcibly reminded herself, she honestly didn't want a relationship with a man, *any* man, especially a man who played with toys. Besides which, she was hopefully about to become involved in something that concerned this man's company, and she had a professional obligation to remain objective. The caller had told her that he didn't know who he could trust in the company, and she had to surmise that that included the president too. And there was one other thing—something was troubling her, but she couldn't seem to put her finger on what it was.

He smiled. "To show you what a nice guy I am, I won't even try to talk you into letting me come to your house. You can follow me back to my house."

"Zach—"

He drew her closer to him and stared down into her eyes. "Apparently you're used to men taking *no* for an answer, but I can't. I want to get to know you better, Cassidy. I want to know what you do for a living. I want to know what you were like when you were a little girl. I want to know what brand of toothpaste you use. Now, I'm positive I'm making a lot of mistakes with you, but there doesn't seem to be any help for it. As I said, I'm strongly attracted to you and have been ever since I first laid eyes on you. But I also know that I'm feeling something more than mere attraction. And whatever it is, it's the reason I walked across my living room last night to meet you."

Cassidy was silent for several long moments. "Has anyone ever told you that you don't play fair?"

He seriously considered her question, then answered her as honestly as he could. "No."

She shook her head, amazed that there really was such a man as Zach Bennett walking around on the earth. A man with eyes that could befuddle a perfectly sane woman's mind with their humor and their dreams. A man who wore a Mickey Mouse watch. "Will we be alone?"

"No, my housekeeper lives with me."

She was going to go with him, she thought, surprised and disgusted at herself. But on the other hand, she rationalized, maybe it was a smart move to get him out of the park. The man who had contacted her might not have arrived yet. "All right, Zach, I'll follow you in my car. But I can't stay long."

With a smile of satisfaction, he put his arm around her, and they started walking toward the exit.

And in the shrubs, behind the bench, there was a sneeze.

Three

"Be sure you rinse those mugs out when you get through with them."

Cassidy stared transfixedly at the woman who had spoken. She held a tray with two mugs of hot chocolate and a plate of cookies. As she deposited it on the cocktail table, Cassidy realized she was the woman from the night before who had offered meatball hors d'oeuvres, the woman who had worn the leotard. Tonight she was wearing a floral housecoat, hoop earrings, and go-go boots. Zach had introduced the woman to her as Lily, his housekeeper.

She raised a warning finger to Zach. "I don't want to wake up in the morning and find chocolate glop in the bottom of the cups. You don't pay me enough to clean chocolate glop, you know."

"I'll rinse the mugs, Lily."

"You better." She straightened and cast an

interested gaze over Cassidy. "You're really pretty, sugar, but you're way too pale. Some blusher, maybe a blend of two or three shades of eye shadow, the right color of lipstick, and you'd be a new woman."

"I—I'm sure you're right, but I thought I was going out for just a few minutes tonight. I didn't expect to run into Zach." The unexpected was becoming the norm since she had met Zach, she thought ruefully.

"I have a shade of lipstick guaranteed to frizz Zach's hair. It's called Scarlet Passion, and anytime you want to borrow it, just let me know."

"Thank you. That's very kind of you."

Zach's gaze met Lily's. "Good night."

"I'm going, I'm going. Now sugar, be sure and have your fill of the cookies. They're Zach's favorite. Chocolate chip with macadamia nuts. He goes into withdrawal if he doesn't have them at least once a day."

"Good *night*, Lily."

She ignored him and continued addressing Cassidy. "Why don't you stop by one afternoon, and I'll do a complete make-over on you. I'll give you a whole new look."

"You do and I'll feed your go-go boots into the disposal," Zach said mildly.

Lily snorted. "Men! They don't understand that the only females who are natural beauties are those who are under five." Those words delivered, she sashayed out of the room.

"She likes you," Zach said. "I can tell."

"She's really your housekeeper?" she asked, thrown.

He smiled understandingly. "She's my very own Auntie Mame with a vacuum cleaner. Sixteen years ago when I started my company, she was my first secretary. The thing was, she couldn't type or take shorthand. *I* was having to do my own typing. But the plants flourished, and the files were always in perfect order. And she made hot cinnamon rolls from scratch which I became addicted to." He shrugged. "I decided to bring her home with me. I wouldn't trade her for anything."

Cassidy nodded, while her mind raced. Lily might be eccentric, but she had acted as a buffer between Zach and herself. With Lily's departure, Cassidy began to grow antsy. The room suddenly seemed smaller, the couch they were sitting on, shorter. She squirmed, shifting her position several times, trying to put a little more space between them.

"Have a cookie," Zach said.

Humor ran like warm honey in his voice; it glided along her nerves, arousing, irritating. "Most men serve wine and fruit to a lady they're trying to seduce—not hot chocolate and cookies."

"Damn, I get that wrong every time."

"I'm serious, Zach. Whatever plans you have, you can forget them."

"Is that why you think I brought you here? To seduce you?"

She stared down at the tray. "Yes . . . No." She sighed. "Maybe." He could scramble her brain waves until there was no chance of intelligent, rational thought getting through. She rose and put some distance between them.

Watching her, he settled himself deeper into the couch and crossed his legs. "Whatever you decide, I'll be glad to oblige. Just let me know."

Ignoring his offer, she found herself in front of a shelf display of O gage trains. A brass plaque below it read "circa 1911." "You must like trains. You have one set up in your bedroom."

"I do like trains. I run the one in my bedroom practically every night. Its sound puts me to sleep."

She glanced around at him, her forehead wrinkled. "Its sound?"

"If I'm having trouble sleeping, the sound of a train is better than any sleep machine I've ever heard. Anytime you'd like to try it with me . . ."

"I think that's bizarre, and I've never had any trouble sleeping," she said, lying. The minute she laid her head on the pillow, her mind came vividly awake with worries, real and imagined.

She bit at her lip and moved on around the room, stopping at another display. This display, marked 1881, held a set of mechanical circus toys. She stared at the acrobats, animals, and clowns, wondering what Zach wanted from her. It was part of her job to be suspicious and look for all the angles, and she couldn't help but examine his reasons for following her. There was no doubt the attraction between them was powerful, and she supposed his reason could be that simple. On the other hand . . .

Suddenly she knew what had been troubling her. Zach had made the observation himself in the park. Twice he had shown up in the place of the man who had called her. Twice he had interfered with her plans to meet the man. As far as she was concerned, *twice* was more than a coincidence. It was time she remembered she was a reporter and did some probing of Mr. Zach Bennett.

She swiveled to face him and strove to keep her tone light. "So is tonight an example of the way you usually operate when you're interested in a woman?"

"Tonight?"

"You know, follow her, badger her into coming home with you, then ply her with hot chocolate and cookies."

He grinned. "Not really. It's just that you're a more difficult case than most."

She blinked. She had known he was confident. Now she added egocentric to his list of characteristics. "It sounds as if you're used to having women throw themselves at you."

His grin widened. "Yeah, but it's never been a real problem. Their bodies pile up around here like cords of wood, and every so often, Lily sweeps them out. Those circus figures move, you know. All you have to do is use the hand crank—"

"I can't believe you're so cavalier about the women who develop crushes on you," she said, outraged.

He pushed himself up from the couch. "And I can't believe you didn't know I was kidding. You need to learn to lighten up a little, Cassidy."

Bobby said the same thing to her all the time.

Apparently it was true. Apparently it was also true that Zach could distract her with the ease of a con artist. She fixed her attention on the ringmaster who was standing on the center platform, his whip in his hand. "Tell me about your company. How deeply involved are you?"

"Deeply."

She jumped at the sound of his husky voice. He had come up behind her without her knowing it. She edged away from him along the shelves. "What I mean is, do you actually create some of the toys, or are you involved more in the administrative side of the business?"

He followed her. "I'm involved in all aspects."

"Well, for instance—"

He brushed his fingers over her blond head. To her overwrought senses, it seemed as if he was comforting her.

"I'll tell you anything you want to know, Cassidy, but first I'd like to know some things about you. For instance, what do you do for a living?"

It was a fair question, she thought, and not overly personal. She felt safe in answering it. "I'm a reporter for the city paper. I've worked there ever since I graduated from college."

"Really? I'm impressed. Do you have your own by-line? Would I have read anything you've written?"

"Probably not." Having told him her profession, she didn't want to go any further. At this point, it was best if she kept his knowledge about her to a bare minimum. She had learned at least one thing about him. Beneath all that lazy charm and boylike dreaminess, he was tenacious. The less he knew the better.

"What about your life outside the office? Your family?"

She shook her head. "I'd rather not talk about that."

"Why not?"

"It's too personal."

He put his hands on her shoulders. She didn't react. He waited, willing her to look up at him. Slowly she lifted her head, her gray eyes cautious. "And what we did last night wasn't personal?" he asked gently.

She stepped away from him, unwilling to risk another one of his kisses. Her concentration scattered, she forced herself to focus on the shelf in front of her and a cast-iron fire-fighting pull toy that consisted of two galloping horses hauling a wagon with a large hose wheel. The plaque read 1895. Curiosity got the better of her, and she touched the wheel. It moved.

"You can take it down if you like. These toys may be antiques, but you can still play with them."

"I'm too old to be playing with toys." And so was he, her tone of voice implied. She felt her back warm as he came up behind her. The heat emanating from his body blocked common sense and acted as some kind of weird truth serum—before she knew it, words came tumbling out of her mouth. "My family consists of my brother. My father left us after my brother was born. My mother died when my brother was eight." She stopped, appalled that she had said so much more than she had intended.

"You have a brother. Great. What's his name? How old is he?"

She wasn't looking at him, but she could smell his scent. Was it a light, citrus-spiked aftershave? Whatever, it made her think of how his hard body had felt against hers as he had held her last night and pressed her against him. Before she could stop herself, more information erupted from her. "His name is Bobby, and he's sixteen."

"I'd like to meet him."

Protecting and guarding Bobby had been her job practically from the day he was born. On that day, their father had left home, and too soon after the birth, their mother had had to go to work. Cassidy had kept all her dates away from the house in order to shield Bobby. The exception was the man she had fallen for when she was in college. She hadn't wanted Bobby to become too attached to any of those men and get hurt when the relationship didn't work out. "He stays pretty busy, what with school and basketball—"

"Does he have a game tomorrow night?"

"No," she said, anticipating he might want to go.

"Good, then I can meet him when I pick you up for dinner."

She hadn't even seen the trap. She turned, her eyes wide with annoyance. "I haven't eaten so much as a cookie with you. What makes you think I'm going to have dinner with you?"

He grinned and lightly touched her cheek. "I guess I'm just an optimistic kind of guy."

The man was definitely dangerous. She forced a smile. "Let's return to the subject of your toy company, shall we? I'd really like to know more."

"Sure. But first, why don't we go back and sit down and have some of Lily's hot chocolate? She'll be crushed if you don't at least take a few sips of it."

She tucked a lock of hair behind her ear and glared at him. "You said you'd tell me anything I wanted to know."

"Where did that accusing tone come from? You're acting as if this is an interview. Is that what it is?"

"No, of course not," she said quickly, and felt a pang of guilt at lying. Why on earth couldn't she maintain her objectivity?

He framed her face between his two big hands and leaned down to her. "Cassidy, I'll talk to you until the sun comes up, on any subject you choose, especially if it's about me, because to my way of thinking that means you're as interested in me as I am about you."

The guilt grew stronger. She was deceiving him, leading him to believe she could grow to care for him—She stopped herself mid-thought. Or *was* she deceiving him? Could it be possible she was already well on her way to caring for him? The very idea was paralyzing.

He nudged her in the direction of the couch. "Then come on. I want to finish my hot chocolate and have a cookie or two. I haven't had my fix for today."

Those twinkling eyes of his were going to be the death of her, she thought, rather dazed. Back at the couch, she reached for her mug and drank. The chocolate was still hot and fortifying. Zach was a grown man whose fondness for toys went beyond his business—surely not the most dependable type of person. And she absolutely *couldn't* be falling for him, and what's more she *wouldn't* let it happen.

Out of the corner of her eye she saw him munching on a cookie. Crumbs clung to the side of his mouth, making him look as adorable as a little boy. Her heart softened. Well, hell. "Your company is privately owned, isn't it?"

"Yes, it's all mine. Have a cookie." He held one out to her, and she had no choice but to take a bite. "Good, huh?"

"Very good," she admitted, chewing. "Now, you started the company right out of school, didn't you?"

He chuckled. "Cassidy, you're asking me questions that you apparently already know the answers to."

She groaned inwardly. He was right. A rank amateur could do a better job of getting information out of him than she was doing. But he had a way of upsetting her pulses, not to mention rearranging her mind. Reflecting on her problem, she took a drink of the hot chocolate, and then set the mug on the cocktail table. Tomorrow, she'd start tracking down all the financial information she could on him. . . .

He leaned toward her and kissed her, stunning her with the gentleness and the unexpect-

edness of the move. His mouth brushed hers,
then his tongue skimmed the outline of her lips.
Heat flared in her stomach, clouds drifted into
her brain. His taste was sweet and sensual, a
combination of cookies and hard arousal. She'd
never known anything like it and eagerly
strained against him, kissing him back.

He lifted his head before she was ready, but he
kept his mouth a breath above hers. "You had a
hot chocolate moustache," he explained, his
voice low and rough edged. "It's gone now."

"Oh." She couldn't think of anything else to
say. No man had ever kissed a hot chocolate
moustache off her lip before. She searched her
mind for another question she could ask, something that would help her find out what was
going on in his company, something that would
get her mind off the shockingly eager way she
had just responded to him.

But then he kissed her again, pushing her
backward onto the couch pillows and easing
over the top of her.

He really hadn't brought her here to seduce
her, he thought, and he didn't plan to now. But
her femininity undid him. And watching her all
evening without touching her had been torture.

Everything he was growing to love about her
she did unconsciously. He was fascinated by
her guarded questions, amused by her disdain
for his toys, captivated by the way she responded to his embrace.

He craved her—it was as simple as that.

Thrusting his tongue deep into her mouth, he
was rewarded by the touch of hers. Then her

arms slipped around his neck and her fingers threaded up into his hair. With a shudder, he pushed her T-shirt up and closed his hand around her breast. Her nipple tightened and pearled in his palm. Blood rushed hotly to his head; excitement pounded through him at a dizzying speed. He heard her make a soft little sound, felt her shiver and lift her hips against him. At the contact, heated desire stabbed through him with bone-searing force.

He couldn't wait any longer to sample her sweetness. His arms corded as he supported himself and bent his head to her delectable breasts and their nipples. He circled one hard, pink point with his tongue, then drew it into his mouth and sucked. Rivers of fire braided through his stomach and down into his groin, and he knew his control was in grave danger of slipping its leash. He returned to her mouth, kissing her again and again.

She was drowning in an ocean of sensual pleasure, and she didn't want to be saved. His mouth had awakened nerves all over her body and taken her past the point where she controlled anything, much less her own responses. Her senses were being swamped by feelings, each one more powerful than the last. And Lord help her she wanted more.

His body was hard and hurting. She was all heat and silky softness and pliable willingness. He wanted her so much, he was half-crazy with it.

But she wasn't his yet.

The thought hammered in his brain, demanding his attention. It was a painful thought, an almost unacceptable one—and it wouldn't go away.

Reluctantly, he lessened the pressure of the kiss until he could make himself break fully away from her. Then, knowing he couldn't continue to lie over her without taking her, he straightened and combed shaking hands through his hair.

She sat up slowly, her expression confused, her eyes still glazed with the desire he had created inside her. "Why did you stop?"

He turned his head and looked at her. "Because," he said huskily, "you never would have forgiven me if I hadn't. You're not ready."

The next morning, Cassidy gave a desultory spin to a pencil and watched it twirl around and around on her desk, unaware of the curious glances from her co-workers. From the time she left college she had been able to handle men. She had received her education about the opposite sex from Gerald Merrick, the man she had fallen in love with and had dreamed of marrying. He had let her down badly, and since that time she had dated only when it was convenient for her, and had never again entertained the idea of becoming serious about a man.

But now Zach Bennett had come into her life. And she didn't have a clue what to do about the way she reacted to him. It was as if she had some strange strain of flu that made her weak beneath his kisses and feverish at his touch.

Whatever it was, this morning she was having to face the shattering truth that she would have made love with him if he hadn't stopped.

The phone rang and she reached for it, wondering where she could get a vaccination for the Zach Bennett flu. "Cassidy Stuart."

There was a sneeze. Then, "There'll be no more meetings. I'm through trying."

"Give me one more chance. I promise I won't mess up."

"No way." He sneezed again. "You're too close to Bennett, and he scares me. Good-bye."

"Wait! Don't hang up. Hello?" The line went dead. "Damn!" She replaced the receiver and stared at it. He was scared of Zach. Why? Did he think Zach was secretly involved in a plan to sell his own product? She supposed it wouldn't be the first time the head of a company sold something under the table for quick cash. And if he were overextended and needed capital, this would be a *lot* of quick cash that could go straight into his pocket without his having to pay taxes on it. She supposed it was even possible the product might be insured in some way.

She didn't want to think Zach was capable of doing such a thing. She almost couldn't believe it. But she also couldn't get past the fact that this man, whoever he was, was afraid of Zach—who had twice intercepted her as she was about to meet her informant. Until this moment, she had forgotten last night's resolve to look into the financial status of both Bennett Toys and Zach. For some reason that had nothing to do with professionalism, she really didn't want to delve into Zach's personal affairs behind his back. But on the other hand, a major theft such as this one in a local company would affect a great many people, and she didn't feel as though she could simply forget the story.

The phone rang again and she eagerly answered. "Cassidy Stuart."

"I just wanted to make sure you remembered that I'm picking you up tonight at seven-thirty."

"Zach?"

"You sound funny. Who were you expecting?"

"No one." Another lie. She had hoped it would be her contact calling her back.

"Are you having a good day?"

She looked at the pencil. "Great, simply great."

"Good, then I'll see you tonight."

"Tonight?" she asked, her mind disturbingly blank.

"Tonight. Seven-thirty."

"No, wait—" The line went dead. Cassidy stared at the receiver, feeling a sense of déjà vu. Everyone seemed to be hanging up on her today.

At seven-thirty that evening, when the doorbell rang, Cassidy was still in the bathtub. Annoyed that she was running late and Zach was on time, she threw the washrag into the water. Why did that stupid Mickey Mouse watch have to work so well?

"Bobby," she yelled. "Answer the door, then go do your homework."

"Okay," he yelled back.

Quickly she climbed out of the tub and toweled off, then went into her room and began to sort through the clothes in the closet. She had no idea what to wear since she didn't know where they were going, but she eliminated everything red and finally chose a silky ivory skirt and blouse.

She was dreading this evening with Zach. She hated duplicity of any kind, especially her own. And she didn't like the way her intelligence and resolve deserted her whenever she was around him. But one way or the other, she seemed to have committed herself to this date, and she was determined to make the best of it. The financial data she had requested on Zach hadn't come back yet. She would keep her wits about her tonight and take every chance she could to get more information.

With Lily in mind, she carefully applied her makeup and combed her hair. Heaven forbid Lily should have more cause for complaint. Then bracing herself, she left her room.

A small monster truck with big fat wheels whizzed by her toes as she stepped into the living room.

"Wow, look at that baby go," Bobby said gleefully, sitting cross-legged on the floor, holding the remote control unit to the car.

"Yeah," Zach said, sitting beside him, his large frame folded into the same position, "and wait until you see what this one does." Using the remote control unit in his hands, he stopped a small blue race car, pushed a button, and popped the hood.

"Awesome," Bobby said.

Zach nodded his head. "Yeah."

"What's going on here?"

Bobby glanced up, a smile wreathing his face. "Look what Zach brought me, Cass. Not only do the headlights work, but the turn signals do too," he said, happily demonstrating the fact.

Anger began simmering, low and furious in her. "I told you to answer the door, then go to your room and do your homework."

"Yeah, but—"

"No buts. I have half a mind to ground you, young man."

"Cass, I've already done my homework."

"That's not the point."

"What *is* the point, Cassidy?" Zach asked quietly from his position on the floor. "Didn't you want him to get to know me?"

His pinpoint-accurate assessment of the truth made her more than a little uncomfortable. "I certainly didn't want you to try to bribe him with—with *toys*. Besides, he's way too old for toys anyway."

"Aw, Cass—"

"It's all right, Bobby," Zach said, his tone mild. "I see the problem. She thinks these cars are regular toys, when they're not at all."

She frowned. "Of course they are."

He shook his head firmly. "Actually they're educational toys, great for teaching physics. For instance, a bigger object has the potential to do more work or have more energy than a smaller object. But a moving object has more energy than a still object." He set his little race car in motion toward the larger truck. "Watch carefully," he said, deliberately crashing the race car into the truck and sending the truck rolling. "And now you see a practical example of the law that says energy is neither used up nor destroyed. So when the car hit the truck it gave it some of its energy."

"Awesome," Bobby said.

Cassidy crossed her arms over her chest. "Sneaky, Zach. Very sneaky."

She stayed angry at herself all evening for getting so uptight over Zach's gifts of the remote control cars. She had acted as if he had given Bobby a do-it-yourself atomic bomb kit. Despite her resolutions, she had once again overreacted to something Zach had done. And it was time she did something about it or got out of this situation completely.

They had dinner at a small, quaint restaurant, and at her suggestion ended up at his house for coffee. He had been surprised at her suggestion—in a way so had she—but his house was full of clues about the real Zach, whom she needed to know so much more about.

"I made those," Zach said, indicating with a wave of his hand the wooden toys on yet another set of shelves in his living room. "And they're arranged chronologically. The first I made when I was about four years old. The last one on the shelf I finished two weeks ago."

He walked over and took the first toy off the shelf. It consisted of a small square block of wood set atop a larger, more rectangular block of wood with four wooden wheels, all held together with dowels. But it was definitely a car.

"You made that? It's wonderful."

He grinned. "I had help and inspiration from the handyman who worked part time on my father's estate. He was an old man named Henry, and he always had plenty of time and patience for me. Practically from the time I could walk, I'd follow him around with big round eyes, watching him fix and put together things with his tools. I wanted to be just like him."

She turned so that she could see his face. "You didn't want to be like your father?"

"My father was and is a good man. He's retired now, and he and Mother still live on the estate. But he was a banker. When I was growing up, he worked away from the house, and I could never see any actual product of his work. I could with Henry's work. He taught me all the basics, and I took it from there." He replaced the little car.

Her eyes went to the last toy on the shelf, an intricately carved and complicated pulley system. "I'd say that was an understatement. Henry would be proud of you."

He laughed. "Yes, I think he would be."

"And your parents?" she asked curiously. "Are they proud of you?"

"They always have been. My dad helped me set up a workshop in the attic when I was seven, and each year added to the tools I could use. It's never seemed to bother him or Mom that I've never stopped playing with toys."

She heard no censure in his voice, but her

conscience was nagging at her. She passed a hand over her forehead. "Look, I should apologize for making such a fuss about the remote control cars."

"You don't have to. I think I understand."

She was caught off guard by the expression of kindness she saw on his face. The expression made her say more than she had intended. "You may, but I still want to explain. I was eleven when my father left us and my mother had to go to work. Someone took care of Bobby while I was at school, but when I came home, he became my baby. I adored him. And when Mother died eight years later, he became mine legally."

"How old were you?"

"Nineteen."

"An eight-year-old boy must have been a big responsibility for a nineteen-year-old girl."

"I would have fought anyone who tried to take him away from me." She made a vague gesture. "I'm a little fierce when it comes to him and trying to get the best for him."

"He's lucky to have you."

She chuckled. "There are times I'm sure he doesn't think so."

"I doubt that. Anyway, thank you for telling me about Bobby and you. Now I understand a little more."

She looked at him oddly. "What? What do you understand?"

"Why my toys bother you. You've had a hard life and never had a chance to be a little girl and learn to play."

She frowned, unhappy with the picture he

had drawn of her. "Just because I took care of Bobby doesn't mean—"

"Lily went to bed early tonight, to get her beauty sleep, she said. I'll go make us some coffee." He leaned down and kissed her. "Be right back."

She watched him leave the room, the frown still on her face. He had a way of slipping under her defenses and making her feel vulnerable, and at the same time, making her feel safe—the most hazardous of combinations, she thought, and shivered.

Her gaze traveled slowly around the room, stopping when it got to a briefcase sitting on a table. *Zach's* briefcase. Slowly she crossed the room to the table and stared at it. Going through other people's possessions was abhorrent to her. Besides, what if she found something that would incriminate Zach, something that would link him with the plot to sell the video game? She turned away. She didn't want to know if it was true. She twisted her hands together. But with her contact out of the picture and Zach her only lead, if she did look in the briefcase and found nothing, she could drop the assignment with a clear conscience.

She silently cursed. The damned thing was probably locked anyway. She turned back, drew the case toward her, and pressed two buttons. The locks clicked open. With another curse she opened the briefcase and started sorting through its contents.

"Looking for anything in particular?" Zach asked, standing in the doorway, his hands in his pockets, the twinkle gone from his eyes.

Four

Ice slid down her spine as she turned to face a Zach she hadn't seen before. His easygoing nature had vanished. A powerful tension radiated from him, making him appear to Cassidy formidable and intimidating, with an anger that bothered her all the more because it was so controlled. But despite his foreboding appearance, she wasn't afraid of him. Somehow she knew without a doubt that he would never harm her.

"Well, Cassidy?"

She faltered.

His gaze steady on her, he crossed the room and shut the briefcase, his movements precise and contained. "You owe me an explanation."

There was no excuse she could give for invading his privacy, searching through his briefcase—no excuse, just the truth. And to tell him the truth she had to decide if she could trust him.

She gazed up at him. Many times she had rued the twinkle in his eyes, but now that it was gone she felt a kind of cold emptiness in her. A simmering anger had replaced his twinkle and behind the anger there was pain.

Pain? *Oh, Lord, she had hurt him.*

Her heart began to ache. And in that moment, she knew.

"I'm sorry," she said, meaning the apology with everything that was in her.

"Just exactly what is it you're sorry for, Cassidy? For being caught?"

"For a lot of things, but especially for not knowing until this moment that I could trust you."

He stared down at her for a long moment. "Are you going to explain that?"

She nodded. "Yes. Let's go sit down, and I'll tell you everything."

On the couch, she clasped her hands together and tried to compose her thoughts. Zach took the decision about where to begin out of her hands.

"This has to do with that man you've been trying to meet, doesn't it?" he asked quietly.

"Yes. He contacted me at the newspaper and said he has information about your company."

"*My* company? What about it?"

"You're developing a new video game?"

"Yes," he said, frowning.

"Well, someone in your company is planning to steal it and sell it to a firm overseas. The man I've been trying to meet with heard a telephone conversation between the two parties involved.

He wanted to give me the information so that I could investigate."

He was off the couch and across the room before she had time to blink. He paced a few steps, then turned to face her, his body rigid. "And you waited this long to tell me? It never occurred to you that I might be even mildly interested in this information?"

"I wasn't sure about you. My contact is afraid of you."

"*Afraid* of me?" He cursed.

"I thought it best to wait and see what I could find out before I decided when and if I should tell you." She hesitated. "I didn't know whether I could trust you or not."

His expression was bleak as he gazed at her. "I built my company from the ground up, Cassidy. All my dreams are in it. Why on earth would you think that I would do something to jeopardize my dreams?"

If at that moment a hole had miraculously appeared she would have gladly crawled into it. Even though one part of her still considered her rationale sound, another part of her felt like a fool for ever having suspected him. "For the very reason that the company *is* your dream. If you were in financial trouble, the sale would offer you quick money."

"I'm surprised you didn't run a financial check on me." His tone was tinged with cynicism.

She swallowed. "I did, but I haven't received the information yet."

His head jerked back as if he had been struck.

"I'm sorry," she said again. "The company might be your dream, but being a journalist is mine. I had to work my way through school, and it took me longer to finish and made me late starting my career. And even after I was able to secure a position with the newspaper, I had to turn down any assignments that would take me out of town because of Bobby. I'm twenty-seven, and I'm still trying to prove myself." She paused. "It's not an excuse, Zach, it's an explanation. And if I had it to do over again, I'd probably do the same thing."

His eyes were enigmatic as he studied her. After a minute, he strode back to her and came down beside her on the couch. "All right, Cassidy, tell me what you know."

"I've already told you just about everything. You spoiled the two meetings that the man set up—another reason, by the way, that I was suspicious of you."

"Both times I was there because of you."

"But I wasn't sure."

"What could I have done to make you sure, Cassidy? Make love to you?"

Unable to hold his quiet, steady gaze, she looked away. "No, you were right. I wasn't ready. I'm *not* ready." She glanced down at her hands, which were twisted together. "Could we get back to business, please?"

"Business. Okay . . . you have no idea who this man is who's been trying to meet with you?"

"None. I assume he's one of your employees. At least, he was in the building when he overheard the conversation. Plus, he said that he had duties he had to perform at the party."

"There were quite a few of my people who donated their time for the party."

"Do you know of anyone who works for you who's afraid of you?"

He gave an impatient shake of his head. "Of course not."

He bolted off the couch again and wandered aimlessly around the room. Finally he stopped before a display of Tootsietoy "aeroplanes" marked 1940 and stared at them. "When is your next meeting with this man supposed to take place?"

"It's not. You really spooked him."

He glanced at her. "You mean he's broken contact with you?"

She nodded. "He hung up on me this morning and hasn't called back."

He picked up a silver and blue plane and flicked the propeller, sending it spinning. "So you thought you'd come here tonight and see what you could find out."

"Basically," she said. Her feelings of shame made the admission grudging.

"And your coming here had nothing whatsoever to do with me, personally, or anything you might feel toward me."

She opened her mouth, then closed it again, unsure how to answer. She had told herself the only reason she was going on this date with him tonight was to see what she could find out. But deep down she hadn't believed herself, not for a second.

He looked at her. "Well?"

"This is all really complicated, Zach."

"Apparently so." Holding the little plane, he flew it through the air in front of him, banking it against the shelves, sending it into a steep dive, then bringing it back to his chest level. "So what's your next step, Cassidy?"

"I don't have one," she said with a frown, wondering why he was playing with that stupid airplane. "I don't have any leads. As far as I'm concerned, the story is dead."

He replaced the plane on the shelf and switched his attention to another shelf and a wooden fort marked 1941. He began rearranging the lead soldiers in front of it. "Do you usually give up on things that easily?"

"It's not a matter of giving up—" Consternation furrowed her brow as she watched him play. "Are you listening to me?"

"You have my complete attention, Cassidy." He rolled a cannon to a different position. "If it's not a matter of giving up, what is it?"

"Well—"

"I thought you said you had things to prove. I'm surprised you get any stories the way you go about it."

He was right, she thought. This story had been important to her, yet she had already abandoned it. But she wasn't sure what else she could do.

He pushed an armored car with an antitank gun in front of a line of soldiers. "I assume your editor is in on this."

"Yes," she said, searching her mind for another tack she could try for the story. "He gave me a week to come up with something, otherwise I'm back in assignment rotation."

"Really? And you don't want that?"

"No. I want my own story with my own by-line."

He began to rearrange the line of soldiers again. "You think the man who contacted you works at my company?"

Playing with the toys was obviously causing him to lose his train of thought, she reflected, because she had already answered that question. "It makes sense." She paused as suddenly a new possibility occurred to her. "I wonder if it would do any good to spend some time—No, probably not."

His expression inquiring, he turned to her, a soldier in his hand. "What were you going to say?"

She shrugged. "Nothing."

"No, go on. I'm interested."

"Well, I was just wondering if it would do any good to spend some time at your company. It might scare the man who tried to contact me even more. But on the other hand, I doubt if he's going to call me again anyway—"

"Let's call him Deep Teddy Bear."

She blinked. "Excuse me?"

"This mystery contact of yours needs a name. I think we should call him Deep Teddy Bear."

"You mean like the Watergate informant, Deep Throat?"

"Not really. They didn't have a Deep Teddy Bear. We do."

She rubbed her forehead. "Are you saying I *should* spend some time at your company?"

"Why not? Can you think of anything better?"

"Well, I—Won't people think it's strange that I'm there?"

"Not at all. We'll tell them you're my new girlfriend."

Her jaw clenched. "Are your employees used to you taking your girlfriends to work with you?"

"Sure."

"Do you do it often?"

"All the time."

Her eyes narrowed. His mood had lifted considerably, and she wasn't certain why. "I don't know, Zach. . . ."

"What have you got to lose?"

He was right once again. "You wouldn't mind passing me off as your girlfriend?"

He smiled. "It would help me, and I could have my secretary give you a list of the people who came to the benefit here. If nothing else, you could talk to them and see if any of them sound familiar."

It made sense. "All right, then. I'll try it for a couple of days."

"Good."

"Good," she repeated without knowing why, noting with both relief and misgiving that the twinkle was once again back in his eyes.

The next morning she stopped by the newspaper to check in with her editor and to pick up her messages. There was no word from Deep

Teddy Bear, as Zach called him. But there was the financial report she had requested on Bennett Toys and Zach. She tossed the report into the trash can, then stood there, staring down at it, chiding herself. If anyone else were involved but Zach, she would read the report without a qualm.

Her face set with determination, she rescued the report and read it. Both Bennett Toys and Zach appeared solidly and healthily in the black. She threw the report back in the trash can, feeling really awful for having read it. What's more she hadn't gained an ounce of respect for herself as a professional journalist. She couldn't seem to win.

Cassidy used the drive to Bennett Toys to think over some things that had been bothering her, namely why she had such a hard time keeping her head out of the clouds whenever she was around Zach. He wanted her. He wasn't the only man over the years to make it clear he wanted her, *however*, he was definitely the only man who had ever made her want him to such an extent that she had no power over her own responses.

Her reaction to him was a *big* problem. And she had committed herself to spending several days with him. A *bigger* problem.

If she ever decided to let herself fall in love—and of course, she told herself, she had no intention of doing so—it certainly wouldn't be with someone like Zach Bennett. Just because he was a nice man and he was an expert at kissing . . .

On the other hand, he hadn't done one single thing to hurt her. And simply because she had had to work hard most of her life didn't give her a right to be judgmental about someone like Zach whose life had been easier. Sure, he played with toys and kept stuffed animals on his bed and wore a silly Mickey Mouse watch, but that didn't necessarily mean he was undependable. After all, he was obviously capable of competently running a large corporation.

No, the problem was with her. She had to get her feet back on the ground and view her association with the toy company and its president as an impersonal assignment.

She was frowning harshly as she turned into the parking lot of Bennett Toys.

"We call this the pit," Zach said to Cassidy, pointing toward the large open area where about twenty people worked in front of video display terminals. "And"—he grinned as he turned to the four people who had just walked up—"these more or less reputable-looking people are the supervisors for our new video game." He gestured toward an attractive brunette who was dressed in a white silk shirt and narrow black skirt with smart gold earrings at her ears. "Cassidy, this is Janet McCloskey. She's in charge of Part One of The Game, The Quest, in which the hero must find a special treasure."

Cassidy smiled. "Hello."

Janet eyed her curiously, but nevertheless

nodded pleasantly and extended her hand. "Hello."

"And this is Will Frazier," Zach continued, gesturing toward a young man who wore jeans and a *Rocky Horror Picture Show* T-shirt and held a box of cough drops. "He's in charge of Part Two, The Battle, where good fights evil. If it is played correctly, not only does good win, but the hero also wins the fair young maiden."

Will's expression was blatantly admiring as he shook her hand. "Nice to meet you, Cassidy. Would you care for a cough drop?"

She smiled, noticing the deep huskiness of his voice which spoke of a cold. Janet had the same quality in her voice. "No thank you. Nice to meet you too."

A man, thirtyish, dressed in an Italian designer suit and mongrammed shirt didn't wait for Zach's introduction. "Hi. I'm Brad Monroe. It's a nice surprise to have you with us today. We're running a special on spice tea that's chock-full of vitamin C. Could I get you a cup?"

"Maybe later."

"Brad's in charge of the last part of The Game, Part Four," Zach explained, grinning at Brad's eagerness. "But I want you to hear about The Game sequentially, so we'll skip to Mitchell Compton, who has Part Three." He indicated an older man with a receding hairline and a thickening middle who wore slacks and a dress shirt opened at the collar.

Mitchell extended his hand with a friendly smile. "Part Three, that's me. It's called The Rescue, which is where evil forces steal the maiden away, and the hero tries to get her back. Pretty much like everyday life."

Everybody laughed, and Zach said, "Okay, Brad, now you can tell her about Part Four."

"Right. I have The Odyssey, in which the hero and the maiden travel back home to their enchanted kingdom, fighting evil forces along the way, kind of like the freeway at rush hour." He fished a handkerchief from his pocket and blew his nose.

"Well, it's very nice to meet all of you," Cassidy said, "and I think it's fascinating that each of you has designed a part of this new game."

Will beamed as if she had given him an exclusive compliment, then he coughed. "The Game is really Zach's baby. He gave us the overall outline, character sketches, and specs, and we just basically filled them in."

Brad nodded and blew his nose once more. "Zach's the brains and heart behind The Game, and it is truly amazing. It's at least a couple of generations ahead of anything on the market today with three-dimensional, high-definition graphics. The rules are different for each section, and the player will have to figure out those rules. There are monsters, tests, magic—" He broke off to cough.

"Not only will the characters in The Game change and grow, but the kids playing The Game will advance in their knowledge as well," Janet said, "because there is a learning system written into the program. But it isn't obvious. As if by accident, their knowledge of things such as geography, history, math, and mythology will grow without them even realizing they're learning."

Cassidy looked at Zach. "You didn't tell me that."

He shrugged. "We haven't really talked about it."

Janet held a tissue to her nose and sneezed. "Despite the fact that we've all been sick, the project is almost finished. About all that's left to do is put our four parts together with the master disk."

Cassidy eyed the four with sympathy. "You've *all* been sick."

Will, Janet, Mitchell, and Brad nodded in concert.

"The whole company has," Will said.

Brad made a face. "Except for Zach."

Mitchell took a cough drop from Will and popped it into his mouth. "But we're getting better. The cough is the last to go. That and the scratchy throat."

Zach rolled his eyes. "I can't tell you how glad I am to hear you're getting better. Cassidy, you've never seen such long-suffering people in your life."

Janet's expression turned to one of mock affront. "Excuse me, but it was the *men* who were babies about the whole thing, not me. In fact, I'm the only one who hasn't been to the doctor or lost a day at work. Everyone knows that women deal with sickness better than men."

Brad looked at Will, then Mitchell. "I didn't know that. Did you guys know that?"

Will and Mitchell both chuckled and shook their heads.

Zach laughed. "As I said, I'm glad you're getting better."

They all seemed so nice, Cassidy thought. It didn't seem to her as if any one of them could be the person Deep Teddy Bear had overheard. "Janet, what is the master disk you referred to?"

"It's what's going to make The Game so spectacular that it will bring our competition to their knees. It's the actual program that will weld our individual four parts into a complete game."

"All we have without the master disk are four video games," Will said, with a deferential look at Zach. "Granted, they're above-average video games, but it's nothing compared with what they're going to be when they're put together."

Mitchell cleared his throat and took another cough drop from Will. "Zach felt it would be easier for us to work on the individual parts this way, and I suppose it was a good security measure too. Right, Zach?"

"Right." He put his hand on her back. "We're on our way over to check out production, so we'll see you later."

Cassidy collapsed into a chair in front of Zach's desk and rubbed her eyes. "I've seen more toys in these last two hours than most people see in a lifetime. And"—she eyed her surroundings incredulously—"there're more in here!" Toys of every kind and color vied for space with file folders and computer printouts in the large, luxurious, sunshine-filled office.

With a wry grin, Zach dropped down into his big leather chair and rested his elbows on the heavily upholstered arms. "What can I say? It's home."

She laid her head against the back of her chair and eyed him curiously. How could he remain so inherently masculine and in control, surrounded as he was by toys, dolls, and stuffed animals? "You're not one bit tired, are you?"

"I make those rounds every day, Cassidy."

She thought for a minute. "Your employees all seem to like and respect you a great deal."

"Well that's good, because I like and respect them."

He was serious, she realized. It hadn't been a throwaway line.

Just then an older woman wearing a shirt-waist dress, her silver hair drawn back into a bun, walked into the office carrying a tray loaded with drinks, sandwiches, and fruit. "Here's your lunch, Zach."

He gave his secretary a smile and rolled a big red fire engine to the side of his desk to make room for the tray. "Thanks, Marsha."

After Marsha had left, Cassidy pondered a stuffed monkey hanging by his hand from a file basket. "What are all these toys, anyway? I mean, does your company sell them?"

"Some of them. Some of them are prototypes. Some of them are sold by our competitors. Some of them are from my personal collection."

She frowned, still not understanding. "But

what are they doing in here? I mean, this is your office. This is where you *work*."

"The toys are here because I like them, Cassidy. Tuna sandwich?"

She nodded absently, reflecting on what she had seen and done this morning. Bennett Toys was even larger than she had believed it to be, spread out over several acres like a college campus. The production plants were housed in several huge auxiliary buildings, and Zach had seemed determined to show her every inch of each of them, right down to the basements, and even one subbasement they were about to seal off. The offices were in the main building, where they were now. And in between the buildings, there were pretty ·little lakes and parks, designed, she had learned, by Zach for his employees' enjoyment.

That Zach could design lakes and parks wasn't the only thing she had learned about him this morning. She had seen firsthand the keen interest he had taken in every aspect of the business. A dirty cog warranted as much of his attention as a doll that didn't have enough hair. He had spoken the truth when he had said Bennett Toys was his dream.

Who was trying to take his dream away from him?

She took a bite of the tuna sandwich. "This is very good."

"I'll tell Lily you liked it. She makes my lunch every day."

"She's obviously crazy about you."

"Yes."

The dreaminess and the twinkle were back full force in his eyes, texturing and deepening their blue color. She squirmed beneath his gaze. "Exactly how many people have access to The Game?"

"The four supervisors you met. Janet, Will, Brad, and Mitchell are each responsible for their individual part of The Game. Each part is on a three-and-a-half—inch disk. At the end of the day each disk is backed up onto another."

"So there are eight disks in all?"

"That's right." He set aside the sandwich he had been eating, pulled the fire engine in front of him, and began cranking out the ladder to its extended length.

She watched, perplexed that he would start playing while they were supposed to be working out a problem together. "And where are the disks kept at night?"

He rotated the ladder, positioning it so that it rested against the file tray. "They are brought to me or Marsha and put into a safe. Only Marsha and I have the combination."

"Could Marsha—"

"No. Absolutely not. She took Lily's position here and has proven herself completely trust-worthy over the years."

"Okay, then, that leaves the four supervisors. Copying his or her own disk would be no prob-lem, of course. The trick would be to get hold of the other three."

He walked a small plastic fireman up the ladder to the top and left him there so that he could look down into the file tray. "It's hard for me to suspect any of them. They've all been good hard workers."

She glanced at the fireman, perched atop the ladder, then she watched Zach pull a little hose from a wheel at the side of the fire truck. Why did he *do* things like this? "Zach?"

His blue gaze fixed on her. "Yes?"

She sighed. "Nothing." She looked around the room and saw a baby doll with a sweet face lying on top of a mahogany credenza. "What about nighttime security? Does anyone ever come back at night to work, and would you know if they did?"

He shook his head. "I don't believe in over-time, and we have a security team that guards the building at night. It would be very hard."

"Hard, but not impossible?"

"Nothing's impossible, Cassidy. But I think the copies would have to be made sometime during the day."

"Okay." She glanced again at the baby doll. "What does that doll over there do?"

"Nothing. She's a doll."

He fastened the fire hose in a miniature fire-man's hand, walked him up the ladder, and there improvised a hand-off of the hose to the other fireman.

Before she could catch herself, Cassidy raised half out of her seat and looked into the file tray to see if there really was a fire. Feeling foolish, she quickly sat back down again. "You know what I mean? Does she eat, wet, cry, suck her thumb, something like that?"

"She doesn't do anything. She's an old-fashioned baby doll that looks as close to a real baby as we could make her."

She frowned. "So what's a little girl supposed to do with her?"

"Love her and play with her as if she's her own baby. Didn't you ever do that when you were a little girl?"

"I—I can't remember."

"Want to play with her?"

"Heavens, no!"

"Just asking." He and the little fireman at the top of the ladder aimed the fire hose at the file tray, and with a *shooshing* noise, extinguished all the imaginary flames.

Cassidy watched, bemused.

When he was through, he walked the two firemen back down the ladder, rolled the hose up, cranked the ladder back to its original position, and finally placed the two firemen in the front seat of the fire truck.

Fascinated, Cassidy noted the concentration he gave to the task. What was he thinking about? she wondered. Was he really *that* caught up in the little game he was playing? She soon had her answer.

"Whoever is trying to steal The Game very likely has already copied the four parts."

Cassidy blinked, wondering what she had missed. "Why do you say that?"

"Because I noticed several things that were slightly out of place when we came back from our tour of the plants."

"How could you tell?" The office appeared a

jumble of confusion to her, with toys filling up all the spare spaces.

He grinned, reading her thoughts. "I have a methodical mind as well as a creative one. I know where everything is."

"Okay, Marsha could have—"

"She's learned never to touch my things. It's one of the reasons she is so valuable to me. Besides, she took an early lunch."

Cassidy wasn't certain she was following his reasoning. "Okay, things were out of place here in the office and that means . . ."

"It means the person already has the copies of the four disks. The person would have to have them before discussing such a big money deal with a buyer. Now the thief is trying to find the master disk."

"Where is it?"

"Someplace very safe." He sent the fire engine rolling across his desk. "You and Bobby will have dinner at my house tonight."

Her eyes widened, startled. "We will?"

"Yes."

She was losing the battle inches at a time, she reflected. Worse, she had become unclear about exactly what the battle was, or why she was fighting it.

Five

Cassidy gave her brother a smile, part wry humor, part chagrin. "Bobby, will you please tell Lily and Zach that I occasionally *do* feed you."

Looking up from his plate in surprise, fork in hand, Bobby asked, "Is something wrong?"

Lily was standing by his chair and patted his head. "Nothing is wrong. You just keep eating."

He grinned. "It's all really good."

Cassidy shook her head in amazement. "If I ate half of what he does, I'd weigh a ton."

Zach chuckled. "Teenage boys need a lot of fuel."

Lily added another roll to Bobby's plate. "It does my heart good to see someone enjoy his food so. There are times Zach would forget to eat if I didn't shove a plate in front of him."

Cassidy looked at him, inquiring.

He shrugged. "I get involved."

"He's always making things," Lily said, adding

a large dollop of mashed potatoes to Bobby's plate.

"What do you make, Zach?" Bobby asked. "Toys?"

He nodded. "I mess around with ideas. Some of them end up to be prototypes. Some don't."

"It'd be great if you could show me sometime how to make something, a really cool car maybe."

"I'd be happy to." As soon as he said the words, he saw Cassidy tense, and he silently cursed. He had hoped by having Bobby with her this evening, she would be able to relax and enjoy herself.

"Your schedule is already pretty full, Bobby," she said carefully.

"Not that full."

"You should see Zach's workshop," Lily said to him. "He has every tool imaginable, and he can work with just about any material."

"It sounds awesome. I'd love to see it."

Zach smiled at him. "Any time."

Cassidy spoke up quickly. "Bobby is going to study engineering in college."

"What kind?" Zach asked Bobby, but his gaze remained on her. She looked so lovely, her blond hair shining in the light of the chandelier. She hadn't wanted to come, but he had insisted. Continuing to get his way with her, he suspected was going to be difficult. Somehow he had to discover who was trying to steal a game that would mean hundreds of millions to his company, and at the same time, win the heart of a woman who had long ago decided to keep her heart to herself.

"Mechanical engineering, I think."

Zach nodded. "It's a good field."

"I'm hoping to get a basketball scholarship.
I'm the youngest player on our school's varsity
team, but Cass says I really shouldn't pin my
hopes on it."

"Your sister may be right. Athletic scholar-
ships are getting harder and harder to come by."
As attuned as he had become to her, he sensed
some of the tension ease out of her. It was habit
for her to protect Bobby in every way she could,
he realized. It was also habit for her to guard her
heart. But whether she knew it or not she was
capable of great love, and he had decided he
wanted to be the recipient of that love.

She smiled at her brother. "Athletic scholar-
ships bring a different kind of pressure that I
don't want you to have to deal with. Basketball
is for fun, period. Grades are for real. And I'm
going to put you through college myself."

He sent a grin toward her that was filled with
loving indulgence. "I know, sis."

Lily slapped Bobby on the shoulder. "How do
you feel about seven-layer chocolate cake, young
man?"

His grin widened. "Are you kidding? I'm very
pro—chocolate cake."

"How did I know you'd say that? Want to leave
the old folks here and come out to the kitchen
with me? We can have some cake and milk and
talk basketball."

"You like basketball?"

"I have an autographed poster of Michael
Jordan over my bed."

"Wow. Can I see it?"

"Yeah, and then we can try out my new skateboard."

He glanced down at her go-go boots. "You skateboard?"

"I've won our neighborhood skateboarding olympics two years running."

"Well, let's go then!" He pushed back from the table. "See you later, Cass, Zach."

"Bobby, it's dark outside—"

Lily gave a dismissive wave of her hand. "Don't worry, sugar. Zach has the best-lit driveway in town. All the kids come over and use it."

"Okay, but we can't stay late. Bobby has school in the morning and a game tomorrow night. And if they win that game—"

"Tomorrow night's game is in the bag," Bobby told Lily and Zach.

"—then they'll have a series of games to play in the state capital."

"The *state* tournament," Bobby said proudly. "I'm already packed."

"That's great," Zach said, sincere in his praise.

Lily hit Bobby on the shoulder. "Yeah, maybe someday I'll be asking you for your autograph."

"Heck, I'll give it to you now."

"Will you?"

"The point is," Cassidy said, feeling like a wet blanket, but unable to help herself, "Bobby needs his rest."

Bobby's voice took on a wistful tone, the same tone that nine times out of ten guaranteed him his way. "We can stay one more hour, can't we, sis? Just to have some cake and ride the board a couple of times?"

"Well . . ." She had given it her best effort, Cassidy thought wryly.

"We'll either be in the kitchen or outside," Lily said, pushing Bobby in front of her and out the door. "Zach, serve Cassidy some coffee and cake."

Once Lily and Bobby had gone, Zach shoved his plate out of the way and leaned back in his chair. "He'll be fine, Cassidy."

"I know he will."

"You're worried about something. What is it?" She didn't answer him. She seemed to be drawing a cloak of self-protection around her.

"I don't know," she said finally. "I guess I'm just preoccupied with whether or not I'm going to be able to get a story out of whatever's going on at your company."

The story wasn't what was bothering her, he thought. At least not at the moment. He needed to get her to talk to him, not about what was happening at the company, but about what was going on inside her. "You're worried about being alone with me, aren't you?"

She looked at him in surprise, her expression unknowingly revealing that he had been right. "No, of course not."

He smiled. "Yes, you are. You thought Bobby's presence would act as a shield. I'm sure in your wildest dreams you never figured that Lily would kidnap Bobby for some nighttime skateboarding."

How could a man who played with toys be so

intuitive, she wondered, her lips twitching with reluctant humor. "No, I didn't."

He tilted his head to one side, considering her. "You're sitting there with some kind of armor wrapped around you to protect you from me, and I don't know why you feel you need it, what it's made of, or what to do about it."

"You do pretty well without knowing," she murmured, grasping a silver knife and drawing a line in the tablecloth.

"I don't even know what that remark is supposed to mean," he said, baffled.

It meant that her insides heated at a mere glance from him. "Didn't Lily say something about coffee? I can serve us if you'll show me where it is."

"I'll get it in a minute." He rested his forearm on the table and leaned forward. "Tell me, Cassidy. Tell me why you've got your arms held out, holding me off, and I haven't attempted so much as to touch you tonight."

She sighed, glanced at him, then dropped her gaze back to the knife. "Actually I've already told you, and you didn't listen. But the truth is, I don't want a relationship with you or anyone."

"I heard you at the time. I hear you now. But what I want to know is *why?*"

Her fingers tightened around the knife's hilt. "It's simple. I've always found it better to go it alone."

"Maybe that was because you've had to."

"No. It's because I've *wanted* to."

"Okay, then, let me repeat my original question: *Why?*"

The knife slipped from her fingers to the table with a dull thud. "I'd really like a cup of coffee, Zach."

He reached across the table and grasped her wrist. "And I'd really like an answer. What you're saying doesn't make sense. You've obviously decided you can trust me, because you've told me about the theft that's about to go down."

"That's business, Zach. What you want to know is personal."

"If you can trust me with the business information, you can trust me with things that are personal."

She shook her head. "I don't see it that way, and I think it's time Bobby and I left."

"No. Not until I have an answer. Cassidy, every time we kiss, it's like instant combustion. The problem comes when we're not kissing. You become guarded and cautious and try your best not to let me touch you."

She eyed her wrist pointedly. "I don't seem to be doing too good a job, do I?"

"Cassidy."

She exhaled heavily. "All right, all right. Just sit back, will you? You make it hard for me to breathe when you're close."

"That's very interesting," he said softly, but he did as she asked.

She passed a hand across her forehead, trying to clear her mind of Zach and his nearness, so she could tell him the story he wanted to hear. The tactic was only partially successful. Her mind cleared, but her body remained tantalizingly aware of him. "I told you that I became Bobby's legal guardian when I was nineteen."

He nodded. "Yes."

"I was already in college then, and working. And I met this man. He was a professor, and his name was Gerald Merrick."

The fingers of his hand slowly curled inward until his hand was a fist, but his tone continued to be soft. "You fell in love with him?"

"Yes I did." Her face took on a distant expression as she cast her mind back to that time. "I thought he was wonderful, and I wanted him to think I was wonderful too. Our dates started out at the local coffee shop, but we quickly dropped the coffee shop as a meeting place in favor of his apartment. I didn't have a lot of free time, but I stole what I could. A really nice lady watched Bobby for me, and I was blissfully happy. Then one day Bobby was sent to the hospital from school with appendicitis, and he had to undergo an emergency operation." She paused, her eyes clouding as she remembered. "I was so scared, and I was all alone. After what seemed like forever, the surgeon finally came out and told me Bobby was going to be fine."

"That must have been a relief."

"It was, so much so that something sort of short-circuited inside me. And all the fear I had been holding in and the relief I felt that it was over got the better of me, and I broke down and began sobbing. The doctor told me to go home and get some rest or I was going to end up in the bed next to Bobby's."

"I hope you did."

She shook her head. "I just couldn't make myself go home to an empty apartment and be alone. I desperately needed to be held and reassured and loved. So I went to Gerald's." She looked at him. "I guess you know what happened next."

"Why don't you tell me," he said gently, the knuckles on his fisted hand nearly white.

"There was another girl in his bed, of course, and I was completely blindsided." Her voice cracked, but she went on. "It never occurred to me that he didn't love me as much as I loved him. It never occurred to me that he wouldn't be there for me when I needed him."

She fell silent, and when she didn't continue, he said, "I'm sorry you had to go through that."

She laughed with deliberate lightness. "That's what life is about, isn't it? Lessons? That particular lesson taught me never again to need or depend on anyone."

"You sound very hard, Cassidy, but I don't believe it for a minute."

Her eyes narrowed on him. "Believe it. I've done very well over the years without anyone."

"I believe that part. I only have to look at Bobby to see what a very capable and loving person you are. He's a great kid, and you've done a tremendous job raising him. But I'm talking about a whole new ball game now. I'm talking about you and me."

"The same rules apply."

"You're wrong. There *aren't* any rules where you and I are concerned."

Much to her dismay, she could feel herself

begin to tremble. "Zach, you're a very persuasive man. As far as I can tell, everyone in your life seems to adore you, and I'm sure there are plenty of women who would love to be sitting in my place right now, but—"

"Before you start with the buts, I'd like to say something. You once accused me of not playing fair—"

"You don't."

"Neither do you, Cassidy. You're judging me because of something some man did to you years ago. Do you call that fair?"

He was overwhelming her again, sapping her strength with his own particular brand of logic. Irrationally, she felt as if she were now losing by *yards*, rather than inches, at a time. "It's worked up until now."

He smiled slowly. "Like I said, it's a whole new ball game. All I ask is that you give me a chance."

"I'm not sure I can, Zach. I'm not even sure I want to."

"You do, you know. Somewhere deep inside where you can't stop the feeling, you do. And even though you're fighting it, you also may be giving me a chance."

He took hold of her hand again, and heat crawled up her arm. She tried to pull away, but with a knowing smile he held fast.

"Cassidy, sweetheart, please stop fighting me."

She swallowed against a lump of emotion in her throat. "I'll stop fighting you when you stop touching me."

He threw back his head and laughed. "Not a chance."

"Then ditto."

Twinkling lights danced in his eyes. "It's going to be fun, you'll see."

"Fun? *Fun?*" Incredulously, she searched her mind for a proper retaliation, but at that moment Bobby and Lily burst into the room.

"Lily's a skateboardin' maniac!" Bobby said, aglow with admiration. "You should have seen some of the moves she made."

"I showed him my special loop-the-loop where I skate down our driveway and up the side of Mr. Fenwick's garden wall."

"The neighbors love her," Zach said to Cassidy.

Lily suddenly tensed as her expert gaze scanned the dinner table. "Zach, what in the world is wrong with you? You haven't even given Cassidy any coffee or cake. Come on, Bobby. You can help me cut the cake, and I'll give you a big end piece."

"Great," Bobby said, disappearing after Lily.

Zach looked at Cassidy. "Fun," he said softly. "You'll see. You can depend on me."

The baby doll rested against a pile of books on the mahogany credenza. Sitting in front of Zach's desk, Cassidy stared at her, thinking how real she looked. She could see how a little girl could fall in love with its sweet face, soft body, and delicate hands and feet. She switched her attention from the baby doll to Zach. He was reclining in the big leather chair behind his desk, looking relaxed, magnetic, and terribly sexy in gray slacks and a blue open-necked shirt.

"I didn't hear anyone who sounded familiar to me yesterday," she said, "so today I'm going to make it a point to go around and introduce myself to those people on the list Marsha gave me, the list of people who worked the benefit party. Also I'd like to learn more about your four supervisors, as well as the security systems in these buildings."

His forehead grooved with thought, Zach nodded as he pushed a Hot Wheels Custom Corvette back and forth across his desk. "All of that can be arranged."

She studied him for a moment. "You look troubled. What's wrong?"

"I'm having a really hard time believing that Will, Janet, Mitchell, or Brad could steal from me."

"Tell me a little about each of them."

He gave a final push to the small car and steepled his fingers beneath his chin. "Will is a young wunderkind. He came to me straight out of school, and I've never seen anyone more enthusiastic about their work."

"What about Brad? That suit he had on yesterday was an Armani, and Armanis don't come cheap."

Zach laughed. "A dress code never seemed real important to me. I've always told my employees to dress in whatever makes them comfortable. Brad loves designer suits and gold watches. Will loves T-shirts and jeans. Everyone else seems to fall somewhere in between."

"What kind of car does Brad drive?"

Zach made a face. "He just bought a Porsche, but Brad's a good guy, and I can't believe that he would steal simply because he has expensive tastes."

"Why not? People steal for a lot less, believe me."

He smiled at her. "Cassidy Stuart, the cynic."

"More like the realist. Tell me about Janet."

"She's smart and very competent. She's worked for me for five years, and in all that time I've never had a minute's problem with her."

Cassidy pushed herself out of the chair and ambled around the office. "You left out one thing in your description of her. She's attractive."

"You're right. She is."

She glanced at him out of the side of her eyes. "Has there ever been anything between you two?"

"Nothing."

She had stopped in front of the credenza, but his flat tone drew her gaze once again. "Why not? Do you have a rule against fraternizing with employees?"

"No. I've never been attracted to her sexually, that's all."

"Oh." She looked at the doll, wondering exactly *who* he had been attracted to in the past. He had said his employees were used to him taking his girlfriends to work with him. How many had there been? she wondered. Other than normal curiosity, no one had seemed the least surprised to see him showing her around. Apparently he showed women around all the time. Broodingly, she touched the delicate lace trim on the baby doll's dress, then fingered the soft material. The doll was so precious, she thought. She couldn't remember ever having a doll, but she must have. . . .

"Have you ever wanted a baby of your own?" Zach asked.

Her hand jerked away from the doll. "No, of course not."

"Why 'of course not?' Wanting a child is a perfectly normal thing."

She returned to the chair in front of the desk. "I've had Bobby—"

"He'll be going off to college in another year, and you'll be by yourself. You're so young. You could have lots of babies."

Heat flushed up her throat to her face. "I don't *want* lots of babies, Zach."

His shrug indicated she was entitled to her own opinion, no matter how crazy. "I do." He leaned farther back in his chair, kicked his feet up on the desk, and crossed one ankle over the other. "In fact, I want a whole horde of babies."

She blinked. "You do?"

He nodded. "I've got a big house, and I can't think of anything nicer than having every nook and cranny filled with happy, healthy, giggling children."

He'd be a wonderful father, she thought unexpectedly. He had more than his share of patience and humor, and he was gentle. . . .

She mentally shook herself out of her reverie.

"Good luck on finding a woman to give you that horde."

His gaze fixed intently on her, he smiled. "Thanks. I'll need it."

His smile was an assault on her senses and sent tingling warmth through her. She cleared her throat. "Let's get back to Janet. I gather she's single?"

"That's right."

"Do you know anything about her personal life?"

"From all appearances, she doesn't live beyond her income, if that's what you're asking."

"Exactly what I was asking," she said thoughtfully. "Okay, what about Mitchell?"

"Mitchell is as solid a citizen as anyone I know. He has been married to the same woman for years, and has two daughters and a son. The oldest daughter is in college, the second daughter is about to start, and the son will begin next year."

She grimaced. "College is so expensive these days, I can't imagine having to put two kids through, much less three."

"Well if we've got to have a motive for this theft, I'd much rather it be because someone was trying to educate their children than someone wanted a new Ferrari."

"You're not taking this seriously, Zach—"

"Here's that coffee you asked for, Zach," Marsha said as she came into the office, two cups in her hand. "Sorry it took so long, but I had to brew a new pot."

"No problem." He accepted one of the cups and watched while Cassidy accepted the other.

Marsha paused at the door, her hand on the knob. "Do you want me to close this?"

He glanced at Cassidy. She had gotten up once more, leaving her coffee on the desk, and wandered over to the credenza and the baby doll. At this point, he was taking great care not to do anything that would make her feel uptight or as if a trap were being closed around her. "No, that's okay, leave it open." He switched his gaze back to Cassidy in time to see her touch the doll's soft, baby-fine cap of hair. He smiled, then carefully wiped all traces of amusement from his face.

"I take what's happening very seriously, Cassidy. Only I don't want to believe that any of the people I work with on a day-to-day basis would take what is going to be the future of Bennett Toys and sell it, no matter how high the price." He paused. "I guess that's why I keep hoping this is a hoax of some sort."

Without thinking, she picked up the doll and cradled it in her arms. "You can't expect everyone to have the same feeling for your company that you do, Zach." She passed her hand over the doll's head and smiled. It seemed to her as if she caught the scent of talcum. The doll was wonderful.

"Yeah, I guess you're right."

"Of course I am," she said, unconsciously beginning to rock the baby doll. "In fact, your feeling about the company may be your blind spot. You love it so much, you can't imagine anyone doing anything to harm it."

"Anything I love, I love totally."

A sudden insight flashed into her consciousness. Her heart stopped, then after a moment started again with a hard thud. It was the dreamers who fell the hardest, not the rakes. And Zach was a dreamer. He would love only one woman and he would love her well. She found herself envying that woman.

"So what do you think?" he asked quietly, watching her.

"About what?" she asked blankly.

"About the doll."

She looked down at the doll as if she'd forgotten it was in her arms. Hastily she put it back on the credenza.

"Do you think she's going to be a hit with little girls, even though she doesn't do much but look like she needs love?"

Cassidy returned to her chair and reached for the coffee. "She'll probably be a big success."

"That's good."

She frowned at his smug expression. "You can just turn off the twinkling in those eyes of yours right now, Zach Bennett."

He chuckled. "Why, whatever do you mean?"

She glanced around the room, searching for something to throw at him, but all she saw were toys. The phone rang on Marsha's desk outside the door, and she heard Marsha answer it with a low, melodious voice.

"Is Bobby going to be home tonight?" Zach asked, distracting her.

"No," she said. "He has an early game, and then he's going to spend the night at a friend's house. Remember I told you that if the team wins, they'll be leaving for the capital in the morning. He's really excited. He and his friend want to get up and go to the bus together."

"Sounds great. We can go see his game, cheer him on, have dinner, and not have to worry about what time we get back."

"Excuse me?"

"I want to spend some more time with you, Cassidy. Away from here, and away from this damned story of yours."

"I don't have a story yet. . . ." Her words trailed off as she heard a man speaking to Marsha. His voice was deep and husky. She turned in her chair and looked toward the door.

"What's wrong, Cassidy?"

Her frown deepened. "That voice . . . He sounds like the man who called me. Who is he?"

Zach dropped his feet to the floor and straightened. "*Delbert, get in here.*"

A young man of perhaps twenty stuck his head around the corner of the door, his eyes round with apprehension. "Yes, Mr. Bennett?"

Zach waved him in. "Come in."

The young man's gaze went to Cassidy, and he swallowed hard, sending his Adam's apple bobbing up and down.

He entered the office with a slow and obvious reluctance, giving her a chance to study him. He was dressed neatly in jeans and a plain black T-shirt. His face was clean-shaven, and his hair was pulled back in an orderly ponytail.

Cassidy gazed with disbelief at him, because what she saw didn't come close to jiving with the mental picture she had had of him. He was so young! "*You're* Deep Teddy Bear?"

He shifted nervously from one foot to the other. "Ma'am?"

"Shut the door, Delbert," Zach said.

"Uh, sir, I haven't delivered all the mail yet."

"Shut the door, Delbert. The mail can wait."

"Yes, sir." Delbert closed the door, then stood uncertainly, halfway between the door and Zach's desk.

Zach got right to the point. "Did you call Miss Stuart with information regarding plans for a theft of the new video game?"

Delbert cast a sideways glance at Cassidy. "Did she say I did?"

Cassidy had been listening closely to his voice. "It *is* you, isn't it? I had pictured someone much older from the way you sounded on the phone."

Delbert developed an interest in the toes of his tennis shoes, staring fixedly down at them. "Well, ma'am, I've had a cold, and my voice sounds a little huskier and deeper than usual."

"Who *are* you, anyway?"

Zach answered her. "His name is Delbert Houghton, and he's worked in our mail room for about a year."

"A year and a half, actually, sir."

"For heaven's sake, why all the secrecy? Why didn't you just come and tell Mr. Bennett what you knew?"

"Uh, well . . ." He rubbed his nose. "Mr. Bennett's the head of the company, and uh, well, I didn't know him very well, or uh, exactly who I could trust, uh, and so . . ."

Zach sighed. "Sit down, Delbert."

Delbert gratefully collapsed into the chair next to Cassidy's. "Thank you, sir."

"Would you like a soda or something?"

His eyes widened with alarm over the fact that the president of the company was offering him refreshments. "No, sir, I'm fine."

"Good. Okay, then, I want you to start at the beginning and tell us everything you know, including how you happened to overhear the telephone conversation."

"Okay, well, it was after work . . ."

"Go on," Zach said encouragingly.

"And—and I'd gone out to get in my car and go home. But, well, it wouldn't start. So I came back into the building to call my brother so he could come jump-start me, and I went into an office and picked up the receiver of the phone and started punching buttons to see if I could get a line out." He shifted in his seat, clearly gaining more confidence as he went. "Well, one of the buttons I pushed happened to be lit up. I realized my mistake and was about to push another button when I heard the words 'ten million dollars.'" He paused and glanced from Zach to Cassidy and back to Zach again. "I don't often hear anyone speak about sums of money like that, and I don't know, I just hesitated for a second, and then I heard one of the people say that Bennett's new video game was almost finished, and that he would be able to deliver the whole package soon. The other man—he spoke with an accent—he said they would need it in the next eight days for it to be worth their while, otherwise they wouldn't be able to get the jump on Bennett's production schedule."

Zach looked at Cassidy and cocked an eyebrow. "I guess it wasn't a hoax."

A pain stabbed at her heart. *He was hurt.* Now he knew for certain that one of the people he had trusted with his dream had betrayed him. And as Cassidy absorbed the fact of his hurt, her desire to find out who was trying to steal the video game grew, not because the knowledge would give her a good story, but because she desperately wanted to help him.

She turned to Delbert. "What else can you tell us? For instance, you said 'he.' Was the caller a man?"

Delbert shrugged. "He sounded male."

"Which phone did you use?" Zach asked.

"One of the phones in the pit, but I couldn't tell if there was anyone in the offices that open out onto the pit."

"Those are the supervisors' offices," Zach said to Cassidy. "Delbert, did you see anyone afterward?"

"No, sir, and I didn't particularly want to either. I figured they wouldn't be too happy with me eavesdropping like that. I called my brother real quick, and then went outside to wait for him." He glanced at Cassidy. "I thought about what I'd heard all night, and the next morning telephoned Miss Stuart."

For the first time since Delbert had begun

talking, humor returned to Zach's eyes. "You had a hot potato in your hands, didn't you?"

Delbert nodded, relieved that Zach seemed to understand. "Right. I don't want to be in the mail room forever. One day I'd like to get my degree and move on up the ladder. But since I didn't know who I'd overheard, I had to be careful about the toes I stepped on. And I didn't have the nerve to come to you, Mr. Bennett, so I decided to go outside the company to Miss Stuart. I was hoping she could break the story before any damage was done to the company."

"At least you didn't keep the information to yourself."

"I couldn't in all good conscience," he said earnestly. "And I'm sorry I panicked when I saw you two together, but I began to get paranoid. It just struck me as funny that I'd never seen you two together before, and then suddenly you were together every time I turned around."

Zach smiled kindly. "We think it's hilarious too. Thank you, Delbert. And if you think of anything else that might help, or overhear anything else, please come and tell us."

"Yes, sir."

Cassidy waited until Delbert left the room, then commented, "We don't seem to know a lot more than we did before he told us. The mystery of Deep Teddy Bear is solved, but I still need to check up on the supervisors, only now, at least, I'll only have to check up on the three men."

"It could still be Janet. Remember, she's had a cold too."

She nodded thoughtfully. "I guess that's right.

She did sound husky yesterday. Well, shoot. We're back to four." She sighed. "Okay, then, I guess I'd better get started." She stood up, and so did Zach. "I'll go check out the security first."

He came around the desk to her and took hold of her arms. "Be careful. I can't imagine any of them are dangerous, but then it was hard for me to believe any of them would steal from me. And ten million dollars is a lot of money in anyone's book."

Her mouth curved into a wry grin. "I know. Don't worry. I'll be all right. And I won't leave the building without telling you."

"That's good," he said softly. "That's very good."

Cassidy instinctively tensed as she realized the mood in the office had suddenly changed. But before she could react, he lowered his head and kissed her, and the tension drained out of her.

His kisses stimulated her senses, robbed her of strength, stole away her reason. She should hate his kisses, but she was very much afraid she was growing to love them. As soon as he put his lips to hers, problems and objections disappeared. He made her want him, need him. . . .

"Zach?" His secretary's voice came over the intercom. "You have a telephone call on line three."

He gently drew away and gazed down at her. "Go sleuth, sweetheart. I'll see you later."

Six

Cassidy slid into Zach's plans for the evening without objection and without subjecting herself to too much self-analysis about the reason she did. For once in her life she decided to try to relax and enjoy herself. And amazingly enough she did.

She and Zach attended Bobby's basketball game, stayed afterward to congratulate him on his team's victory, and then went out to dinner. She laughed a lot during dinner, but she also gave some consideration to what was happening between Bobby and Zach.

It was apparent to her that they really liked each other. Their interest and affection for each other had been instant, and there'd been nothing she could do to stop it. But, she reasoned, Bobby was older now and would be able to understand the concept of two people working together for a short while, then moving on to other things. Bobby wouldn't be hurt when Zach disappeared from their lives.

The real question was, would *she* be hurt? Since she had met Zach, a different and troubling tension had begun to grow in her. She felt prickly, hot and bothered, and terribly confused.

Zach took her hand as they walked from the restaurant across the well-lighted parking lot to the car.

"Would you like to come back to my house for hot chocolate?"

His question struck her as funny, and she smiled up at him. "You're still pushing that hot chocolate?"

"I'm devoted to hot chocolate. Kingdoms have been lost and won for hot chocolate, not to mention fair young maidens."

Some of her humor faded. "Your tried and true method of seduction?"

One eyebrow cocked as he stared at her. "I'll let you know. Right now, the jury's still out."

She stopped in the middle of the parking lot, her expression one of wonderment. "I have never in my life met anyone like you. I never know whether to take you seriously or not."

"You'll learn," he said reassuringly, and dropped a swift, light, hot kiss on her mouth.

She sighed, feeling very much like a hit-and-run victim. "You're a dangerous man, Zach Bennett, and should probably be locked up for your own safety, not to mention mine."

With a chuckle, he took her arm, and they started walking again. "Everything will be much better once you stop fighting me."

Her hair shimmered in the dim light as she shook her head. "Surrender isn't in my vocabulary."

He grinned. "Then you should be warned, giving up isn't in my nature."

"I was afraid of that."

Reaching his car, he opened the passenger door for her, helped her in, shut the door after her, then walked around to his side.

A small smile curved Cassidy's mouth as she buckled her seat belt and followed Zach's progress around the car. Still absorbed by the warmth of his kiss and his humor, she was caught totally off guard by the sight of two men materializing out of nowhere. Before she knew what was happening, they had grabbed Zach and hurled him up against the car. The car rocked from the impact.

She cried out in horror and reached for her seat belt release, but fright made her fingers clumsy. She could see that one of the men had Zach's arm twisted behind his back and had him flattened against the car. The other man was searching him.

It seemed like forever, but in reality it was only seconds before she was able to unfasten her seat belt. She flung open the car door and bolted out just in time to see the two men throw Zach to the ground and run away.

She raced around the car and dropped down beside him. "Zach, are you all right? Did they hurt you? Did they hit you? Good heavens, Zach, say something to me. Tell me you're all right."

He looked up at her. "I'll be glad to as soon as you stop talking."

She felt like hitting him; she felt like hugging him with all her might. She drew a ragged breath. "Are you okay?"

He sat up slowly. "I'm fine. I've just had the breath knocked out of me, that's all."

With nervous agitation, she brushed some of the parking lot dirt from his sport jacket. "I'm calling the paramedics first, and then the police."

"That won't be necessary."

"Why? They were brutal. Do you know who they were or what they wanted?"

He sat quietly, letting her tidy him up. "I don't know who they were, but I know what they wanted. The disk."

Her hand stilled on his shoulder. "They were after the master disk?"

He nodded. "I'm sure they were hired by the person who's trying to steal The Game. I've been half expecting this. Whoever it is has tried to search my office, but hasn't had any success. I figured sooner or later it would occur to them I might be carrying the disk. A three-and-a-half-inch disk would easily fit into my billfold."

She stared at his calm demeanor in disbelief. "Was it in there?"

"No. Neither was any money or credit cards—purposely. I have an account at the restaurant, and I signed for our dinner tonight. Only my driver's license was in my billfold, and I'm sure they left that. They dropped the billfold on the ground behind you."

She turned, retrieved the billfold, and held it open up to the light. His driver's license was in place. Tears filled her eyes. The attack on Zach had lasted less than a minute, but it had been the worst minute she had spent in a long time, and she still hadn't recovered. Determinedly she blinked the tears away and focused on the picture of him on the license. "This is a really awful picture of you, Zach. You've got the silliest grin on your face, and it looks as if you didn't comb your hair that morning."

"Actually, I don't think I did."

Deeply shaken that someone had hurt him, she lashed out at him. "You were stupid to put yourself in so much danger. If you were expecting this, why didn't you hire a bodyguard?"

"Lily would have wanted the job, and I figured I already pay her enough as it is."

"You're joking again, but this is serious."

He reached out and gently caressed her cheek. "Yes, I'm joking, and yes, this is serious. But being able to see humor in situations that may even be tragic is how people make it through life, Cassidy. It's something you've got to learn." He glanced around the parking lot and moved to get up. "Let's get out of here."

"Wait," she said, worriedly grabbing him. "Don't move. You may be hurt worse than you think. They threw you hard against the car and could have broken some of your ribs. Stay here, and I'll go back to the restaurant and call for a doctor."

"Don't be silly."

Before she could stop him again, he got to his feet. She stood, too, and looked at him with exasperation. "Having a doctor look at you is merely a sensible precaution, Zach."

"It would be if I needed one, but I don't." He put

his hand on the roof of the car for support. "I told you, they only knocked the wind out of me."

"Uh-huh." She took his arm and led him around to the passenger side of the car, where the door was still open. "You're being stubborn and childish about this, but then I don't know why I expected anything less from you. You're an utterly impossible man. Get in. I'm driving, and I'm going to take you home."

He grinned. "Anything you say, Cassidy.

Her arm around Zach's waist, supporting him, Cassidy switched on the hall light just inside the front door of his house. "Where's Lily?"

"She's at her tae kwon do class. After that she's spending the night at her sister's."

"She has a sister?" Cassidy asked in surprise.

"A little frightening, isn't it? Their parents actually produced two of them."

"Never mind. I'll get you to your room myself. Do you think you can climb the stairs?"

"I'll try." He smiled to himself, taking pleasure in the way she was fussing over him. He had told her the truth when he had said he wasn't hurt, and he had had plenty of time to recover his breath on the drive back to the house. But as long as she wanted to take care of him, he was willing to let her.

Up in the bedroom, she switched on the nightstand light, pushed the stuffed toys to one side of the bed, and pulled back the covers. Then she turned to help him off with his sport coat. With a couple of shrugs from him, the coat slipped into her hands, smelling of citrus and Zach. The scent glided past her guard, nearly intoxicating her before she realized it.

"Lie down," she said, more curtly than she had meant to. But he obediently dropped onto the bed. She went to the end of the bed and pulled off his shoes. "I'm giving you your way tonight—"

"That's all I've ever asked."

The look she cast him was repressive. "—but if you are in any pain at all tomorrow, and I don't care how little, just any twinge of pain at all, you're going to the doctor."

"Did you fuss over Bobby's every scratch and cut this way?"

She returned to the head of the bed. "You weren't merely scratched or cut, Zach. Those men threw you up against that car with brutal force. Anyone with a modicum of sense would do the same thing for you as I am."

"Oh, I see." He didn't want to give himself away, but he was hard put not to laugh. Her attention delighted him, but even more than that, his heart filled with love and his body filled with an aching longing as he watched her flutter about, hanging up his sport coat and putting his shoes in the closet. And she looked beautiful and very, very precious as she came down beside him and leaned forward to loosen his tie and undo the first few buttons of his shirt.

"Would you take off my tie, please?" he murmured huskily.

She nodded and stripped it from around his neck. "Is that better?"

"Yes, but could you undo the rest of the buttons on my shirt?"

"Are you having trouble breathing?" she asked, concerned, as she hurried to do as he asked.

"Remember when you told me you had trouble breathing when I was close?"

Her hands slowed on the buttons. "Yes."

"I have the same trouble."

"I don't understand. *Are* you having trouble breathing? Do you need something?"

"Yes and yes." His voice grew thicker with each word. "You." He curled his hands around her soft upper arms. "I need you to touch me."

There was something new in his eyes, she realized, and wondered why she had been so slow to see it. The dreaminess had become focused with desire. The twinkling had changed to fire.

"Zach—"

"There's nothing wrong with me, Cassidy, that you can't fix. I want you in the worst way and have almost from the first moment I saw you. Fix me. Touch me."

She felt herself soften, heat, weaken. Swallowing, she discovered that her throat had become constricted.

He took this initiative and pulled open his shirt.

"Don't do this, Zach." She could barely get her voice to rise above a whisper. "Don't ask me."

"I'm afraid I have to."

"No, wait. There's something you should know. I—I haven't made love since I was in college."

"Cassidy," he said with the greatest of tenderness, "you've *never* made love." He took her hands and brought them to his chest.

Fire scorched her fingertips as her hands splayed over his skin, and her breasts began to swell and throb. She gasped with wonder. "What is it you do to me?"

"I hope it's the same thing you do to me," he said huskily. "Just being in the same room with you makes me crazy. Just looking at you makes me rearrange all my priorities. And always, no matter what the circumstances, you make me want you like I've never wanted anyone or anything."

A helpless sound escaped from her lips. Beneath her palms, his flesh felt hot, and his heart beat strongly in a rapidly increasing rhythm that matched her own heartbeat. Hesitantly she moved her fingers over his nipples and through the fine matting of hair. Then she was drawn back to the fascinating nubs. They were tiny and hard and astoundingly tempting. Surprising herself, she bent down and lathed her tongue around one nipple, exploring the feel and the taste of him. New sensations rocked through her, and her own nipples tightened in response.

He put up with her attention for a long space of time, but then he groaned roughly. "Lord, sweetheart, we're going to have to do something else for a while or I'll have to take you right now."

"What?" she asked with soft bewilderment.

"Kiss me."

His request penetrated the haze of passion slowly closing around her. She knew what happened to her when he kissed her, knew how her control fled and her mind shut down. Some remaining vestige of protective instinct made her shy away from what would surely and ultimately lead her to give herself up to the passion. "No. When we kiss—"

"Exactly. When we kiss the world goes away." He reached up and cradled the side of her face. "Let's make the world go away, Cassidy. We're all alone tonight. Bobby's taken care of. You don't have a worry in the world."

Her eyes clouded. "Yes I do. You. You worry me a lot."

"Why?"

"Because I don't know myself when I'm in your arms."

He eased his hand around to the back of her neck and gently pulled her down until her breasts rested on his chest and her face was close to his. "I know you. You're a woman who's capable of great passion and love, and I want all you've got to give."

Her breath caught in her throat. Her lips moved, silently saying his name. Her resistance and control crumbled, piece by piece.

He lifted his head from the pillow and feathered kisses over her face, her cheeks, her throat, and finally her lips. Delicate, light, exquisitely heated kisses. Soon she began moving her head, anticipating the kisses, without words *asking* for the kisses. And when he slowly lowered his head back to the pillow, she moved with him, not wanting to break the enchanting contact.

"You're mine," he whispered with fierce satisfaction, "and I'm never going to let you go."

She barely heard him. His kisses were stronger now, hotter. And when at last he fully claimed her mouth, she eagerly parted her lips and met his thrusting tongue with hers.

There was heat everywhere. And a driving urgency. In her mind, in her body, even in her soul. When he pulled her over him and onto her back beside him and then began undressing her, she could only rejoice. Their clothes were a hindrance to the total contact she sought.

Suddenly elation rose in her as she realized she wanted so many things: To touch him all over, feel his sleek skin and bunching, rolling muscles. To have him touch every inch of her, exploring, learning, and driving her wild. And most of all, to feel the hard, full length of him inside her.

She was burning with the want, she was *choking* with it.

Clothes were torn and discarded until they were both naked. He pulled her hard against him, and she gave a cry of ecstasy. In the next moment, his hand took possession of her breast, and his mouth came down hungrily on the nipple. A sweet, beautiful feeling pierced through her, carrying a fever with it. She lifted her back, pressing her breast more fully into his mouth. He made a guttural sound, and his other hand went between her legs to the sweet tenderness there.

Her hips began to undulate, excitement spiraled, and the sensations became astonishing and dizzying. Too much so. Not enough.

Her fingers threaded into his hair, holding his head, as he sucked at her breast, pulling on her nipple. Something was happening to her, she thought dimly, something that had never happened before. Every muscle in her body had tightened, and it felt as if all her nerves had risen to the surface of her skin. And in her stomach and between her legs, a fiery tension coiled and twisted and built and built.

He raised himself away and looked down at her. His face was primitive and hard, his blue eyes brilliantly ablaze. "Tell me you want me. Tell me."

"Yes," she whispered. "Yes, Lord, yes. Make love to me." The things going on inside her wouldn't let her give any other answer. There was an excitingly savage quality to his voice, a primal fierceness to his need. And in the deepest center of herself, she was being ravaged by the same needs.

He claimed her quickly and with complete domination, burying himself in her with one powerful thrust. Fire scorched through her, leaving her clinging and shaking. But in the next moment, a strength and urgency seized her, and she arched up to him, meeting his strokes, taking him deeper into her.

This joining was different from what she had known before. It was all encompassing, all involving, as if they were becoming part of each other. Tension and fire clawed at her insides. She whispered his name, instinctively knowing he was the answer.

The spasms caught her unaware. They started and didn't stop, going on and on, hurling her toward a release she wanted, needed desperately, gripping her with a madness and an ecstasy that had no end. She buried her face in his shoulder and cried out his name. He lifted her head and caught the sound with his mouth as he emptied himself into her.

She awoke slowly, feeling a wonderful, floating kind of heaviness. Gathering her strength, she lifted a hand and rubbed at her eyes. Then she opened them.

Black glass eyes stared back at her.

With a gasp, she recoiled, and at the same time came instantly and fully awake. It was the stuffed lion, she realized, and it had apparently been lying eye to eye with her while she slept.

She jerked away, rolled over onto her back, and realized she was holding the giraffe against her. She pushed the long-necked animal away, sat up, and found a cushily fat hippopotamus at her knees.

It was the middle of the night, and she was surrounded by stuffed animals.

And Zach wasn't anywhere to be seen.

With a groan, she buried her face in her hands. What had she done? What had she gotten herself into?

At first she was too upset to move. The very thing she had fought against had happened, and it had happened with an ease that was frightening. What she and Zach had shown each other in incredible physical ways . . .

Staring at the stuffed animals, she tried to think of something else—but her mind refused to cooperate. Zach was the only subject she could think about. And in the end she had to admit that she might not be taking the whole situation so hard if she had awakened in his arms. He would have soothed her, she knew. He might even have made love to her again. Her face flamed at the thought.

Where was he?

She scrambled off the bed. Minutes later, she found a white terry-cloth robe on the back of the bathroom door and wrapped herself in its voluminous warmth. She tied the belt around her waist and folded back the sleeves, then gazed at herself in the mirror. She saw wide, startled gray eyes, tousled blond hair, and a face that had been kissed bare of makeup. And her lips— her lips were swollen from even more kisses, deep, soul-shattering kisses. Amazingly the overall effect was one of softness. She looked relaxed, she thought soberly, and she looked satisfied.

She lifted the robe's collar to her face and inhaled. The robe smelled of him—male, citrus, musk. She knew the scent intimately now. And him. Heat wound through her and tied her lower body into knots at the thought.

Where was he?

The plush carpet rubbed against her bare feet as she turned and went in search of him. She had been in only a few rooms of the house, and fortunately she found him in one of those rooms, the living room. He was sitting cross-legged on the floor by the fire, dressed in sweat pants and surrounded by red building blocks of some sort.

She paused in the shadows of the doorway.

The glow of the fire bathed over him, adding a golden hue to the dark beige-colored skin of his chest and shoulders. It hadn't been that long, she remembered, since she had splayed her hands over his chest in wonder and clutched at his shoulders in rapture.

Had that wanton really been she?

He looked up, saw her, and smiled. "Hi. Come join me."

Feeling awkward and embarrassed, she crossed the room. Going to bed with a man and losing control with said man were not every day occurrences for her. She wasn't certain how to act. And she didn't know *what* to think about finding that said man playing with blocks on the floor in the middle of the night.

She slipped her hands into the pockets of the terry-cloth robe and studied the structure he was building with the blocks. "What are you doing?"

"Nothing much. I couldn't sleep, and I didn't want to wake you, so I came down here."

"And left me with those stuffed animals of yours. They were all cuddled around me. It was sort of weird."

"They're nice to sleep with. They don't snore."

"You do?"

His smile broadened. "You'll have plenty of time to find out, I promise."

Even though she had fallen asleep in his bed, she couldn't envision actually *sleeping* with him. To sleep with someone bespoke an intimacy even greater than what they had shared, and she couldn't imagine it. She sat down on the floor across from him and gazed uncertainly at him from beneath her lashes. "What exactly are you making?"

"It's a castle."

She took a harder look at the structure and realized he was right. He was building a castle that was well on its way to being a fit residence and stronghold for a nobleman, complete with battlements, towers, and crenels.

"Do you want to help?" he asked, watching her reaction.

"No." She wasn't really sure what she wanted. But it seemed absurd to her that she had just had the most passionate sex of her life with this man, and now he was playing with building blocks. Hadn't she heard that most men fell asleep after sex?

"Are you sure? I could use some help with that parapet over there."

"I would get nothing out of building a castle with blocks, I assure you. It looks like a big waste of time to me."

His eyes twinkled. "Is there something else you'd rather be doing? Would you like me to go back to bed with you?"

"No, of course not." The idea aroused her. To cover the confusion she felt, she picked up one of the blocks; it was smooth beneath her fingertips. A closer examination of the blocks revealed they were of all different sizes, shapes, and weights. "What kind of blocks are these? I've never seen any like them before."

He grinned. "They're Bennett Blocks. I designed them. They've been on the market for a few years now and have been a great success."

"But you're just stacking them. I mean, they don't snap together. What's holding the castle together?"

"Learning and faith."

"Excuse me?"

"Children have a lot of limitations in their lives. They're constantly told don't do this, don't do that. With my blocks they learn to have faith that they can do anything they want to do with just a little bit of trial and error, or in adult terms, a little bit of learning. As they play with the different sizes, shapes, and weights of the blocks, they learn which go best together so that they 'hold,' and which will stack on top of another without falling. In other words they learn what works and doesn't work. It's really a lesson in spatial engineering."

"And you designed them?"

He nodded and casually handed her a curved block. "Try that one over there on the corner tower, will you?"

She added the block to the tower. "It's perfect."

"That's good to know."

She felt duped. "Zach, you designed the stupid things. How could you *not* know that particular block would work there?"

He grinned. "I've never built a castle before. I usually build forts. But tonight I felt the need to build something really elaborate. I had a great deal of thinking to do."

"Really?" He had just been inside her. She had dug her nails into his back. But she didn't feel confident enough to ask him what he was concerned about.

He looked over at her. "I've been thinking about the person who's trying to steal The Game."

"Have you had any ideas about who it could be?"

He shook his head. "I haven't got a clue, and part of the reason may be that it's incredibly hard for me to consider any one of them capable of betraying me."

"I'm sorry, Zach."

His expression turned to one of surprise. "For what?"

She shrugged. "I don't know really. I guess I feel badly because I'm the one who brought what was happening to your attention. I was the messenger with the bad news."

"You should feel good about that. By telling me, you're going to be responsible for saving my company an untold amount of money."

"I know, but I'm also responsible for your discovery that someone you trusted betrayed you."

"*Tried* to betray me. They're not going to get away with it."

"I hope not."

"Hey." His tone was whisper soft and so was his touch as he reached across the castle and brushed a finger down her cheek. "Everything is going to be fine."

A sweet, warm feeling crept around her heart. She wished with everything in her that she could believe him. But she still had too many doubts about him and about the two of them together.

"Does this battlement look right to you?" he asked.

She switched her attention back to the castle, reflecting wryly on the difficulty of keeping up with his mind. "It's crooked," she said, eyeing it critically, "and one crenel is larger than the others." She took several blocks from the top of the castle's battlement and began rebuilding it.

A smile played around his lips as he observed her for a few moments. Then he went back to his own construction. "Whoever it is who's trying to steal the master disk has searched my office once—I'm sure they'll do it again—and they've had me searched—"

"Brutalized, you mean."

His mouth twitched. "It really wasn't that bad, Cassidy. Those two guys were no big deal. They were probably hired from "Thugs R Us."

She shook her head impatiently. "I don't understand how you can joke about it."

"It's easy for me to joke about it because I wasn't hurt. And in case you didn't know, I love the way you're so fierce about the whole thing. It shows you're a very passionate woman. Of course, I already knew."

Embarrassment heated her neck and face. In an odd sort of way, it pleased her that he thought she was passionate, but she still couldn't seem to come to terms with her wanton behavior with him in bed.

"At any rate," he said, continuing as though

he hadn't said anything heart-stopping, "I'm sure the next step will be to search the house."

"The *house*." Her eyes widened with realization. Of course. She should have thought of it herself. And she probably would have if she hadn't just spent several brain-melting hours in bed with the owner of the house. "What are you going to do to stop them?"

"Nothing," he said, critically eyeing the castle. "I think I should let it happen. Why not? It won't do any harm. No one will find anything."

"The master disk isn't here?"

He shook his head. "Nope. And if I let whoever it is search the house, he or she might slip up in some way and give us a clue. By the way, your battlement is looking pretty darned good. The thief's time is running short; he or she must be getting desperate."

She exhaled heavily. "You know what I think?"

"No, but I'd love to."

"Even though you're hurt that someone you trusted is planning to steal from you, I think you're enjoying the game of trying to catch them."

His smile told her she was absolutely right.

"I love games, Cassidy, and this game is more elaborate than I'm used to playing. It has a dangerous edge to it, and to make it even better, it's thrown me together with a woman I think is quite wonderful." He paused. "Remember when you came in and I said I was thinking?" She nodded. "It's true I was thinking about the person who's trying to steal the game, but I was also thinking about you." His tone changed, turned lower, huskier, more seductive. "I was thinking of ways I could keep you with me."

Her heart began to pound. "You mean for the rest of the night?"

"For a start." He shifted around the castle until he was beside her. "I want to make love with you again."

Heat radiated from his body and infiltrated hers. "B—But what about the castle?"

He glanced at it, then back at her. "It's finished. We made something beautiful together."

The castle *was* beautiful, she thought, all red and shining, enchanting by the fire's light. "I didn't do much."

"You helped a lot. If you hadn't come along, that battlement would have remained crooked, and the soldier who used the crenel that was too wide would have been a sitting duck against enemy arrows."

"You're joking again."

"Yes, I am," he said, his expression tender. Holding her gaze, he untied the belt of the robe and slid it from her shoulders.

She had only managed to accumulate a paltry amount of resistance against him since she'd awakened with the stuffed animals, and now it began to give way inside her. "Wait. What are you going to do about the castle? Are you going to save it?"

His eyes took on a curious expression. "No, I'm going to take it apart so that I can use the blocks again. Why?"

"It seems sad to tear down something you worked so hard on, and that came out so well."

He smiled slowly. "But look at it this way. Taking the blocks apart will give us a brand new chance to build. Think of the possibilities. They're endless. We'll build many other things together, Cassidy. Better things."

He eased her back to the floor, and she went, her head spinning. Just when she thought she was beginning to understand him, something happened to prove that she didn't. Her lack of astuteness concerned her. But when his mouth touched her throat, then her breast, she forgot about the concern and concentrated on the heat. She had to, because all of her other abilities had fled. His lips carried a magic that she was incapable of withstanding, his touch a sensuality that meant more to her than the dawn of a new day.

"You are so beautiful," he murmured huskily, skimming his hand over her stomach and down between her legs.

Pleasure scorched through her. How had he come to know her so well, she wondered, in such a short time? How did he know exactly where and how to touch her? And how was she ever going to be able to do without him once her story was finished? Her mind fogged over, protecting her from the reality of having to seek answers. She moved against his hand, and when her first climax came, arched her back off the rug.

He was inside her when her second climax came, and her third. Then it was his turn to arch, bowing his back, letting go with a hoarse loud cry.

Seven

Cassidy's internal alarm clock went off at six the next morning, and she awoke to the realization that she was once again in Zach's big bed, a warm, furry kangaroo sharing her pillow. She closed her eyes, then opened them again. The kangaroo wore a happy expression and seemed glad that she had finally woken up.

What's more, her back was cradled against Zach, spoon-fashion, and his arms were tightly around her. She couldn't remember ever in her life being as comfortable, and for a moment she actually considered staying as she was for a little while longer, to savor the unfamiliar experience of being warm and relaxed and held by a man who now knew her body better than she did.

She looked again at the kangaroo. He had kind eyes, she thought. Then her brain clicked into full wakefulness. No matter what her body felt to the contrary, it wasn't prudent to stay in this situation, and she had better at least attempt to get out of it. Trying her best not to disturb Zach, she began to ease out of his arms.

"What's wrong?" he asked, his voice low and husky, his mouth pressed to her ear.

She rolled over to face him and immediately regretted it. His blue eyes held a seductively dreamy expression, and his night's growth of beard tempted her fingers to touch. "I need to get up."

"Not yet." He pulled her naked body against his.

The intimacy and heat nearly swamped her. "I want to go see Bobby's bus off," she said, her breath uneven.

He sifted her hair through his fingers. "Why didn't you say so? I'd like to go too."

"You would?" She wasn't sure why she was surprised. She knew he genuinely liked Bobby, but then Bobby was easy to like. Even so, this time next week she and Bobby would be alone again, and another woman might be here in this big bed. She pushed back from him, putting some space between them, and felt the kangaroo nuzzle her neck.

Zach smiled sleepily, sexily. "I'll give Bobby my good-luck gnu to take with him on the trip. His name is Harold."

"A gnu?"

"Yeah. It's sort of an African antelope with a head like an ox, a short mane, a long tail, and horns. Real cute—"

"I know what a gnu is. But is it stuffed or alive?"

"Stuffed and just the right size for a trip. I think Bobby will like him. Harold and I've been through a lot together, and he's always been there for me."

She sat up, pulling the sheet with her, and noticed three of the stuffed animals clustered around her feet. Her feet had been cozily warm during the night, she remembered. "Bobby won't take a stuffed animal with him on a varsity basketball trip."

"Why not?" He skimmed a finger down her spine.

The warmth made her shiver. "He just won't. He's a jock, and he'd feel silly if his teammates saw him lugging around a stuffed animal."

"Oh." After a moment's consideration, he sat up beside her. "Well, I'll offer Harold to him anyway. Let's get moving and take a shower. I wouldn't want to be late."

She tucked the sheet primly beneath her arms. "You can take yours first. I'll wait until you're through."

"What's the matter with you?" he asked, looking at her with mock concern. "Have you forgotten about ecology and the environment?"

"Eco—?"

He grasped her arm and pulled her out of bed with him.

"Zach, what are you talking about?" she asked, glancing wildly around, looking for something to cover herself with. But all she saw were the stuffed animals gazing sweetly back at her.

He tugged on a lock of her hair. "Gone are the days when any of us in good conscience can take a shower by ourselves. Everyone has to be more ecologically aware. So you and I will take a shower together. That way you can scrub my back, and I'll scrub yours, and we'll save water and time and be able to make love all in one go. It will be a superefficient way to start the morning."

"Zach."

"Yes?"

"Your mind works totally differently from everyone else's."

He grinned and swept her into his arms. "Thank you, Cassidy."

Much to Cassidy's surprise, Bobby loved the idea of taking Harold, the gnu, along with him on the trip. To her further surprise, several of Bobby's teammates approached Zach before the bus took off and asked if they could keep Harold as a mascot for the rest of the season. Zach happily gave his consent, and to give him credit, and Cassidy did, he didn't say I told you so.

After they waved Bobby and his teammates good-bye, Cassidy insisted she and Zach take separate cars to work. It was her way, she supposed, of asserting her independence. And after an assessing moment of thought on his part, Zach didn't argue.

At Bennett Toys, she sat in on a meeting he had with his four supervisors. Even though Zach played with Hot Wheels the entire time, there wasn't a doubt in her mind that he was in complete control of the meeting. Janet, Mitchell, Brad, and Will seemed to hang on his every word, and their obvious respect appeared to be due to more than just the fact that he was their boss. As she studied the supervisors, she tried to put together what Zach had told her about each one with what she was seeing and hearing. But by the end of the meeting she had come up with exactly nothing, not even a speculation.

After they filed out of the office, Zach came around the desk and perched on its edge near her. "Well?"

She lifted her shoulders. "I'm beginning to think you're right. That it can't be any of them. They all seem so nice, and they obviously admire you a great deal." She paused, her expression perplexed.

"What is it?"

"I don't know. There's something bothering me, something I can't put my finger on. They're able to speak better, and their colds seem to be clearing up."

"Yes." He paused. "Is it something about their voices that's bothering you?"

She shook her head and gazed up at him, her forehead creased. "I don't know."

He leaned down and kissed her lightly. "Don't worry about it. I've got a plan. We'll talk about it tonight. But now I've got to go make my rounds of the plants. Want to come with me?"

"No thanks. I'll wait until I'm wearing my jogging shoes so that I'll have a small chance of keeping up with you."

"Did you just make a little joke, Cassidy?" he asked softly, his breath sweet and warm on her face.

She grinned. "Not at all. I spoke the truth, the *absolute* truth, as a matter of fact."

"Uh-huh." He straightened, and as he did, he pulled her out of her chair and up to him, so that she was standing between his knees. "Will you be here when I get back?"

"I'm sure I will be. I want to talk to your head of security some more."

"Okay, then, I'll see you later."

He kissed her again, long and deep, as if he couldn't get enough of her, she thought hazily, wrapping her arms around his neck and kissing him back. Her breasts were pressed against the muscular planes of his chest, and her nipples stiffened and began to ache. His hands slid down her back, cupped her buttocks, and pulled her pelvis tight against the hard ridge of his manhood. Passion flared up in her so fast and so strong, she was shaken when he left.

Deeply disturbed, she leaned back against the desk, waiting for the effects of his one kiss to wear off. He had made love to her all night. She had slept in his bed. He had gotten her to help him build a castle. He had given her brother a stuffed animal mascot for his team.

And he still wanted more from her. What? How much? And most importantly of all, what was it going to cost her to give it to him? She rubbed her forehead. Plainly, she hadn't wanted a relationship, yet he had continued to pursue her until last night when they had set each other on fire with their lovemaking. . . .

He liked to play games, she thought. It was the only answer.

Last night he had linked her and their meeting with the game of discovering who was trying to steal the video game from him. *She* was the game of the week. When the game was over, would their affair end? Feeling strangely depressed, she pushed herself away from the desk and walked out of the office.

Marsha looked up from her work. "Hi, Cassidy. I thought you'd be going to the plants with Zach for his daily rounds."

With a smile Cassidy stopped at the secretary's desk. "I decided to wait here for him. When I went with him before, I came back exhausted."

Marsha laughed. "I know what you mean, but I don't think he'd tolerate the administrative work over here if he didn't have the plants to escape to. He loves seeing the products of his imagination come to life."

"I guess that's understandable."

"Yes." Marsha laughed. "And the people who work over there love him. He's a legend to them. They still talk about the day he invented the Bennett Blocks."

"What happened?" she asked, her curiosity making her edge closer.

"He was over at one of the plants, talking to several of the workers, when he suddenly was seized with this idea. He asked for something to write on, but no one could find a single piece of paper. So he told one of his executives to take off his coat and turn around. The man did, and Zach proceeded to write the specs for the blocks all over the back of the man's pristine white shirt. Everyone gathered around and watched with awe. When Zach was through, he asked the man if he would mind taking off his shirt. The guy went home shirtless with his tie knotted around his neck. It was hysterical. The next day Zach had a dozen new shirts delivered to him." Marsha grinned at the recollection she had shared. "Zach is one in a million, but then I'm sure you know that."

"Yes," Cassidy said faintly. Zach was a man who combined practicality and absurdity with ease and finesse. And his brilliant creativity was matched by his extraordinary capacity for reason and logic. And he left her totally confused. "Marsha, there's something I've been meaning to ask you."

"Sure. What is it?"

"Well, it's just that everyone here has been so nice to me. No one has so much as blinked an eye that I've been hanging around like I have."

"Why should we? You obviously make Zach happy, and that's all we need to know."

It was as Zach had said, Cassidy thought. They were used to him taking his girlfriends to work with him. She shrugged. "I guess Zach enjoys having his girlfriends with him here."

"Girlfriends? Cassidy, you're the first woman Zach has ever brought up here."

"The first . . ."

"Absolutely. It must be pretty special between the two of you."

The first. She felt like shouting "Hallelujah!" But she quickly stifled the urge and her joy. Being the first, she told herself hastily, didn't mean too much in this case. Zach had her here because of the story and for no other reason. And he had let her believe she was one of many as a joke. Zach was always joking.

The phone on Marsha's desk rang, and she answered it. "Mr. Bennett's office. . . . Yes, yes, she is. Just a moment." She covered the mouthpiece. "Cassidy, this call is for you. You can take it right here if you like."

"Thanks." A little puzzled at who could be calling her, she reached for the phone. "Hello?"

"Cassidy, this is Janie down at the paper."

"Oh, hi." Janie was a bright, friendly young woman who had the adjoining desk to hers at the newspaper. "What's up?"

"I thought you'd want to know. We've just had a report that one of the school buses that was on its way out of town, heading for the state capital for the tournament, has been involved in a wreck."

Cassidy went cold. "What school?"

"I'm not sure. At this point, there's still a lot of confusion."

"What about the kids? Any injuries?"

"Apparently so. They're taking them to the hospital now."

"Thanks, Janie." She thrust the phone back at Marsha. "I've got to go." She darted into Zach's office and grabbed up her purse.

"Wait," Marsha called when she hurried back out. "What was that about kids and injuries?"

"There's a possibility that my brother has been in an accident. I've got to go to the hospital."

"What do you want me to tell Zach?"

She hesitated. "Tell him I'll call him when I can."

The trip to the hospital was the worst fifteen minutes of her life. She prayed all the way. Bobby was her whole life, and not knowing if he was hurt had her caught in the grip of the worst fear she had ever felt. Visions of him on a stretcher, covered with blood, terrorized her. "His life hasn't even begun yet. Lord," she prayed, "please don't let him be hurt."

The emergency area of the hospital was in a state of mass confusion by the time Cassidy got there. Ambulances were arriving every few minutes, along with cars carrying parents every bit as frantic as she. All available hospital personnel were busy, and she could find no one who knew anything.

She tried to calm herself and assess the situation. None of the teenagers who were coming in on stretchers looked familiar to her. Thankfully, they also didn't seem to be badly hurt. At last she saw a woman who appeared relaxed standing by a stretcher, talking to the boy lying on it, who was wearing a cervical neck collar.

She walked over. "I'm sorry to bother you, but

could you tell me what high school was involved in the accident?"

"John Quincy Adams High School."

The relief hit her like a blow, and she staggered backward.

"Are you all right?" the woman asked with concern.

"Yes, yes, I'm fine." She attempted a smile. "I'm sorry. It's just that I was so worried about my brother . . . but he attends another school."

The woman nodded. "I understand. I've just spent a hellish half hour myself. This is my son."

This time Cassidy didn't have to force the smile as she looked down at the boy. "How are you?"

Unable to move his head, he made a face. "I'm not hurt. Everyone's making a big deal over nothing."

"He's fine," the mother said. "Just shaken up. As far as I know none of the kids were seriously hurt, but the paramedics didn't want to take any chances with them. All the kids will be x-rayed and observed, but after that they may get to continue on to the tournament."

"That's great. That's really great." Cassidy glanced at the activity around her. "I guess I'd better get out of the way. Thank you for talking to me."

She left the hospital and crossed the parking lot. But once at her car, she leaned back against it. Shock had caught up with her. Her head was spinning, her legs felt as if they were about to give out from under her, and she couldn't seem to get warm. When Bobby returned home, he was going to get the biggest hug he had ever gotten from her, she thought wryly.

"Cassidy, is Bobby all right?" Zach asked, running up to her.

"Yes," she answered automatically, still numb from her recent scare. "It wasn't his school bus that was involved." Then looking at him, her brows drew slowly together in puzzlement at his sudden appearance. "What are you doing here, Zach?"

"What in the hell do you think I'm doing here? Marsha called me over at the plant and told me what had happened. I left immediately. I was three minutes behind you. Why didn't you ask Marsha to get me so that I could come with you?"

"As it turns out there wasn't any need. Bobby wasn't hurt."

"But you didn't know that, did you?" He plowed rigid fingers through his hair. "Lord, I don't even know how you could drive. You must have been half out of your mind. You could have been in a wreck yourself."

His intensity shook her. She had never seen him this serious, not even when she had had to tell him someone was plotting against him. "I *was* half out of mind," she admitted slowly, "but I didn't get into a wreck, and I'm okay now."

He grasped her shoulders. "You're missing the point. Maybe you're *deliberately* missing the point. You know my set up. You know that Marsha can get in touch with me almost in-

stantly. Why didn't you ask her to so that I could
drive you?"

"Because there wasn't any need. I made it just
fine." She tried to shrug his hands away, but he
tightened his hold.

"Dammit, Cassidy, you *are* deliberately missing the point. I should have been with you. If
Bobby had been hurt, I could have helped you,
comforted you."

He had her on the defensive, and she didn't
like the feeling. "Zach, I'm used to taking care of
situations like this by myself. I've done it most
of my life."

"But don't you see that you don't have to now?
You've got me."

"Got you? That's news to me. And then there's
always the burning question of whether I want
you."

He released her and stared down at her, his
face set into harsh, severe lines. "That's it, isn't
it, Cassidy? You *expected* me to let you down,
and so you decided not to give me a chance to be
there for you."

An uneasiness began to infiltrate her already
unbalanced nervous system. "I don't know what
you're talking about. I got the phone call and I
left immediately. I didn't have time to think
about anything but getting to the hospital as
fast as I could."

"Didn't you?"

She frowned. "Didn't I what?"

"Didn't you think about me at all, Cassidy?"

An image of herself as she was about to rush
out the door leaked into her mind. Marsha had

said, "What do you want me to tell Zach?" And she had hesitated. In that flash of a moment, she had thought about him and if she should have him contacted. And she had made her decision.

"You did think of me, didn't you?" he asked quietly.

Looking up at him, she received the second blow of the day. Deep in the depths of his beautiful blue eyes, she saw pain, pain she had put there by her actions. She had hurt him once before by withholding information from him and going through his briefcase. And she had seen him hurt by the thought of someone he trusted betraying him.

And now she had hurt him once again, and the knowledge almost made her ill.

"Do you always flinch long before a blow comes, Cassidy? Because that's what you did. You anticipated I wouldn't be there for you, and you didn't give me a chance to show you that I would."

"Zach—"

"You took the possibility to prove that you were wrong right out of my hands."

She wanted, needed, to say something to him—to defend herself, to help him understand, to help herself understand. But she didn't know what words to use.

He gazed sadly down at her for a long moment, then turned and walked away.

She drove slowly home. Once there she changed out of the skirt and blouse she had worn for work and into a pair of jeans and a pullover sweater. Then she set about cleaning the house. She scrubbed the kitchen floor and vacuumed the living room and bedrooms, She washed and dried clothes. She dusted and polished. And finally when she couldn't find anything else to do, she had no choice but to sit down and reflect on what had happened.

She had always taken pride in how independent she was, in the fact that she and Bobby didn't need anyone else but each other. Granted there had been times over the years when she had felt alone and lonely. She thought back to those frightening nights long ago when Bobby had been sick and she had had to sit up all night with him, trying to get his fever down, trying to help him breathe. But she had managed very well on her own.

Now Zach had come along, cutting smoothly into the center of her life. He had been drawn to her because of that stupid red dress, but he had stayed. He was a persistent man with the ability to focus completely on what he wanted. And he had decided he wanted her; just as obviously at some point she had decided she wanted him. She wasn't sure when she had made the decision, or even why. But she had gone to bed with Zach and loved every minute of it.

She had vowed never to need a man, but her need for Zach was a thing she couldn't seem to control. There was the silliness and the laughter. There was the way she couldn't seem to catch her breath whenever he was around. And there was the rapture that defied description and that, in her whole life, she had only known with Zach. Her clawing, burning need for him made her want to seek protection by running far, far away. The problem was, she couldn't stand the thought that she'd never see him again.

But she had hurt him, and he had walked away from her.

What was she going to do?

She glanced at her watch. It was evening. More than likely he would be at home.

Chewing worriedly on her bottom lip, she ignored the painful knots in her stomach. Would he even want to see her? He had apparently put some sort of trust in her, and without meaning to, she had failed him. She had projected her uncertainties and fears onto him. She had been afraid of being hurt again, so she had taken the safe way out, the cowardly way, and she had rejected him before he could reject her.

She heaved a sigh. As hard as it had been, she had made herself come face to face with the truth of what she had done. Unfortunately, resolving the consequent problems wouldn't be as easy.

She glanced at her watch again, then reached for her purse.

She had to go to him.

Eight

Lily answered the door wearing a housecoat that boasted a palm tree motif. "It's about time you got over here, sugar. I've been wondering where you were."

"Why?" Cassidy asked uncertainly. "Has Zach said anything?"

One penciled eyebrow arched significantly. "Not a word, which has said a lot, if you know what I mean."

"Not really."

Lily patted her on the arm. "Well, never mind. Just go on upstairs. Turn left at the top of the stairs and go all the way to the end of the hall. He's in his study. You two have a good evening. If you need anything, you'll have to help yourself. As they say on *Masterpiece Theatre*, I'm going to retire to my quarters."

"Thank you, Lily. Sleep well."

Cassidy eyed the stairs with trepidation, unsure of what kind of reception she would receive from Zach. Actually, she reflected, she probably shouldn't have come. But she was here now and she didn't want to leave, at least not until she had seen Zach.

She followed Lily's directions to the door of his study and knocked. There was no answer, but she could hear noise of some sort coming from inside the room. She knocked again and waited. When she heard no response, she opened the door and went in.

A big mahogany desk sat angled in the corner of the room against a bank of windows that she knew had to offer a view of the river. A computer sat atop the desk. Books of all sorts plus an extensive collection of antique soldiers lined the wall behind it. A long sofa and two large arm-chairs were arranged at the opposite end of the room in front of a fireplace where a warm, cheerful fire burned. Toys made up the rest of the decor.

And in the middle of the room, Zach sat cross-legged on the floor, engrossed in the elaborate train set spread out before him. He had taken off his shirt and shoes, but he was wearing the slacks he had had on earlier, a white cotton T-shirt, and socks. He also wore a headset that was connected to a state-of-the-art stereo system. And an extraordinarily sweet-looking, two-foot-high stuffed tiger sat beside him.

"Zach?" she said, her voice raised so that he could hear her. His head jerked up, and she saw surprise register in his eyes.

He stripped the headphones from his head and leveled an appraising gaze at her. "I didn't think I'd see you here tonight."

She shrugged uneasily. "I—I wanted to come."

"Why? If you're worried about the story, don't be. Just because we had a personal falling-out doesn't mean you can't be in on the plan to catch the culprit. You'll get your story. You deserve it."

All she heard were the words "*personal falling-out*." He made what had happened between them sound so coldly antiseptic, so final. She felt herself sway and looked around for something she could lean against for support. There wasn't anything. Her tongue flicked over her dry lips. "I wanted to come here tonight to tell you that you were right."

He returned his attention to the train set, flipping a switch so that the train was directed onto a different set of tracks. "About what?"

"I did flinch long before the blow, so to speak. I don't know if I do that all the time, but I definitely did it today." He didn't look up. "I'm sorry if I hurt you, Zach."

He stopped the train and shoved a plump sofa cushion beneath a section of the track, creating a mountain.

She made a sound of exasperation. "Zach, I just said I was sorry."

He was silent for a moment, then he pushed a switch to start the train up the cushion-mountain. "Exactly why did you come here tonight, Cassidy? To say you were sorry?"

"Yes."

"Okay, you've said it."

Perplexed and slightly angry, she crossed her arms beneath her breasts. "You know, Zach, I'm not sure what I expected you to do when I said I was sorry, but I definitely didn't expect you to ignore me."

He turned a knob and the train picked up speed. "I'm not ignoring you."

"You most certainly are. Your whole attention is on that damned train set."

He looked up at her, his expression grave. "*You* have my whole attention, Cassidy, and you have from the first moment I laid eyes on you."

Truth rang from every syllable he spoke, and she felt as if a truck had hit her. She put a hand to her head, for the first time truly ashamed of her stupid prejudice and jealousy of his toys. Lord, what was wrong with her? If she had learned one thing about Zach by now, it was that toys were an integral part of who he was. They helped him think; they gave him pleasure; they provided his engineer's mind with an outlet for the application of science, mathematics, plus creativity; they earned him an excellent living. It had been demonstrated to her time and again that he was one of those rare individuals whose mind could operate simultaneously and brilliantly on many levels, and she kept forgetting it. "I'm sorry, Zach."

"You've said that."

"But this time I'm sorry about being jealous of your train."

He reached over and scratched the tiger behind its ear. "Well, that's certainly a new one.

Aren't you supposed to be jealous of other women?"

"You haven't given me any cause to be jealous of another woman. Only of your toys. But I realize now how silly I've been."

One eyebrow lifted. "Be careful, Cassidy. Admitting that you're jealous implies that you care."

Disturbed by both what he said and the answer she was about to give, she shifted her weight from one foot to the other. "Of course I care. Zach, I went to bed with you. That makes you only the second man in my life I've ever done that with."

"But you were in love with the first man, or so you thought at the time."

"Yes." When he didn't add anything, she said, "So? That doesn't change the fact there hasn't been anyone since him, not until you."

"No, it doesn't." His expression changed to one almost of kindness. "Why don't you sit down, Cassidy."

She dropped to a sitting position on the floor facing him across the intricately woven track system he had laid out. The tracks surrounded a small town, complete with houses, a church, a school, and a town hall. Directly in front of her was the train station with a water tower and a coal bin. "What were you listening to when I came in?"

"A special presentation by the London Symphony. Press that button beside you."

She did, and just in time, a crossing rail raised for the train to speed under. A long space of silence followed. Willing her nerves to calm, she watched the train run its route.

"You're afraid of commitment, Cassidy."

She jumped, startled by his voice. "Commitment?" She said the word as if she had never heard of it before.

He nodded. "You're afraid of it."

"And you're not?"

"No."

She was thunderstruck by his answer. So much so she couldn't think, couldn't immediately come up with anything to say.

"Was there another reason you wanted to see me, Cassidy? I mean, besides to say you're sorry?"

She nodded vaguely, her mind slowly beginning to work again.

"What was it?"

"I—I just wanted to see you."

He stopped the train, checked a section of the track, then started it again.

She watched the smoke curl from the engine's smokestack as the train clicked along the track, up the cushion-mountain, under a chair leg, and around the town. He had said he wasn't afraid of a commitment, but then he had dropped the subject. Had he been referring to a commitment between the two of them? She didn't know. He hadn't mentioned the word love. What was she supposed to think? By his own admission, games could hold him enthralled. And she had to wonder if she was really important to him, or just the toy of the moment.

"*Why* exactly did you want to see me, Cassidy?" he asked. "Have you decided you can trust me?"

Instinctively she took a deep breath, somehow knowing her body was going to need all the life-sustaining oxygen it could get in the next few minutes. He had asked her an important question. Her answer would be even more important. And he wasn't going to like it. "No, I haven't. But then it doesn't seem to matter. I wanted to be with you."

He hit a switch and stopped the train. Supporting himself with a hand on his leg, he leaned toward her, his face taut. "You wanted to be with me tonight? How? In bed?"

"I— I—"

His eyes burned with intensity. "Come on, Cassidy. Tell me. Say it. Did you want more of that sweet, scorching sex we had?"

It felt as if strong, wide bands were constricting her chest, but she forced herself to be honest. "That was part of it."

"Cassidy," he said, slowly, quietly, carefully, "when you take off your clothes and lie down beneath me and open your legs, you are putting yourself in one of the most vulnerable positions you can. Did you know that?"

She swallowed against a hard lump in her throat. "I guess I've never thought about it that way."

"But I'm right, aren't I?"

"Yes." She wanted to look away from him, but the sheer force and power of his gaze held her. It was as piercing and sharp as a laser.

"Have I ever taken anything less than exquisite care of you when we were in bed, or on the floor, or in the shower, or wherever we happened to be making love, tangled up together, sweating and feeling those earth-shattering things we seem to be able to make each other feel?"

"N—no." Much to her chagrin, the memories that his words evoked started a slow burning inside her stomach and down between her legs.

"So then why don't you trust me to be there for you when you need me outside the bedroom?"

She stared at him for a long moment. "I don't know."

His body jerked. Returning his attention to the train, he began adding more cars. She studied the procedure as if her life depended on knowing how to do it. When the train started up again, she followed its progress. It made the circuit of tracks several times, then unexpectedly came to a stop in front of her. She looked at it, then without thinking, reached for the tiny silver scoop in the coal bin and began filling the coal car with the small black chunks that represented coal.

Zach watched her. In her jeans and T-shirt, without any makeup, she looked like a teenager, yet she had carried a heavy load of responsibility from the time she had been a young girl. Her hair fell forward, casting shadows onto her delicate cheeks. Her brow was furrowed with troubled thought. She appeared very fragile and unprotected.

She had been through a lot today, and so had he. She had made him angry. She had hurt him. But if she hadn't come to him, he would have gone to her. And now that she was here, there was no way he was going to let her leave.

He spoke into the silence, his voice soft and husky. "Let's go to bed, Cassidy."

He stood and extended his hand to her. She hesitated for the mere space of a heartbeat before putting her hand in his and rising.

He led her down the hallway to his bedroom. There, standing in the middle of the room, he slowly undressed her. Her T-shirt came off first, then her bra. A shudder raced through her as, unerringly, his gaze dropped to her high, full breasts. He drew a deep, jerky breath, then his hand covered one soft mound, and shortly afterward his mouth fastened onto the nipple. Nerve-altering heat shimmered through her and pooled in her lower body as he drew strongly on the hardened tip. She moaned at the now familiar sensuality that burned along her nerve endings and seared her through and through. And when his hands went to her jeans, she hurried to help.

He caressed and kissed each newly exposed area of skin as if he were discovering her all over again. His mouth could work magic in her, she reflected hazily, his tongue, miracles. Her head fell backward on her slender neck, and she grasped his arms, steadying herself. By the time he skimmed her panties down her long legs, she was shaking and on fire.

He wasted no more time. He lifted her into his arms and carried her to bed. The corduroy comforter and the stuffed animals felt soft beneath and around her. He felt hard as he moved between her legs and entered her. He filled her, he completed her, and he brought her to peak after shattering, rapturous peak.

Cassidy heard a knock from a great distance, but she couldn't seem to respond. Clouds of sleep were weighing her down, pinning her limbs to the bed. The knock came again. She felt Zach stir behind her and realized he was once again holding her against him, her back to his front. Groggily, she opened her eyes in time to hear another knock and see the bedroom door open a crack.

Lily stuck her bouffant-coiffed head around the door. "Oh, good, you're awake." She kicked the door open and entered, carrying a tray which she put on a table at the foot of the bed. "I thought you all would be about ready for a good breakfast." She strode over to the windows and began flinging back the curtains. Morning light flooded into the room.

Panicked, Cassidy sat up and jerked the sheet to her chin all in one motion, sending the hippopotamus and the giraffe tumbling to the floor. The kangaroo stayed stubbornly by her side.

Zach sat up more slowly, cuddling the lion against his chest and eyeing his housekeeper with an amused gaze. "Good morning, Lily. To what do we owe this honor?"

"Oh, I don't know," she said, bustling back to the foot of the bed. "I was just in a French toast sort of mood this morning. You know how that goes."

"Let me guess. You made us French toast."

"Uh-huh." She took the tray, set it in front of Cassidy, then went out to the hall and hurried back with a second tray which she put in front of Zach.

Cassidy stared at her tray and the beautiful presentation of thick-sliced French toast and plump red strawberries. Her tray also held a weird floral arrangement. "It looks very nice," she said, her voice faint with embarrassment.

Oblivious to what Cassidy was feeling, Lily set about with gusto to plump up her pillows and straighten the covers. "Might as well get your daily dose of cholesterol and vitamin C right at the top of the day, that's what I always say. Don't I, Zach?"

He looked over at Cassidy, his mouth twitching with suppressed laughter. "That's what you always say, Lily."

She critically eyed Cassidy's rigid posture. "You'll enjoy your breakfast much more, sugar, if you sit back and relax."

Reluctantly she leaned back against the pillows as directed, careful to bring the sheet with her, covering herself to her neck.

Lily picked up the giraffe and the hippopotamus and set them beside Cassidy, then patted the kangaroo on the head. "By the way, sugar, the flower arrangement isn't edible. My ikebana class is tonight, and that's my homework."

"Oh." It was all Cassidy could think to say as she stared at the small oval dish that held shiny black rocks, three twigs, and a single bright orange daisy.

Zach pulled his tray toward him. "From the looks of that arrangement, you may have a shot at being the valedictorian of your class."

Lily gazed with pride at the twigs and flower. "That's what I was thinking."

Cassidy searched for something to say. "The coffee smells wonderful."

"Freshly ground. Coffee's kind of a family thing with me. Juan Valdez is my second cousin."

"Second cousin? You mean the little guy on television with the donkey and the coffee beans?"

"That's right. He's my second cousin on my mother's side three times removed."

"Juan Valdez isn't a real person, is he?" Cassidy said, whispering beneath her breath to Zach. "I mean, isn't he a symbol for the National Federation of Coffee Growers of Columbia?"

Zach's reply was low and gentle. "Lily should know who she's related to, Cassidy."

While they talked, the object of their conversation had been industriously picking up their clothes, which they had uncaringly left on the floor last night, neatly folding them, and placing them conveniently on the chair, as if it were something she did every day.

When she was at last satisfied that she had everything in order, she clasped her hands in front of her and surveyed them with interest. "Is there anything else I can get for you two?"

"Not a thing," Cassidy hastened to reassure her.

Zach shook his head. "Thanks, Lily."

"No problem. Enjoy. See you later."

As soon as the door was shut, Cassidy groaned. "I can't believe she saw us like this."

"Like what?" Zach asked, taking a bite of his French toast.

"Together. In bed. Naked."

"She meant well, but if it bothers you, I'll tell her not to do it again."

She looked at him uncertainly. "Does she do this every morning?"

He laughed. "Are you kidding? I never get breakfast in bed. No, I told you before, she likes you."

"Oh."

He leaned over and gave her a soft kiss, and his musk and citrus scent encircled her, soothing her nerves and awakening her senses.

"Eat your breakfast," he said huskily.

She picked up a strawberry and nibbled on it. He had said he would tell Lily not to do it again as if he believed there would be many other mornings such as this. The idea pleased her. It also terrified her. And as soon as she had the story, she would have to face and then deal with this surprising and powerful dependency of hers. A dependency named Zach.

As soon as she had the story, she repeated to herself, feeling a new and extremely strong kinship with Scarlett O'Hara.

"Are you coming to work with me today?" he asked.

"I can't think of anything constructive I could do there. I've just about reached dead ends on everything I've looked into. Your after-hours security system is excellent there. I don't see any way it could be violated. And as for the reports I ran on the supervisors, the information I received matched exactly with what you said. There was nothing that would throw up a red flag on any of them."

"But it's definitely one of them."

She glanced over at him and saw that his expression was solemn. "Has something else happened?"

"Lily was out most of the day yesterday. When I came home last night, the key pad of the house security system had been turned off. From the looks of it, the person who disarmed it had an extensive knowledge of how electronics and computers work."

"I gather they didn't get the master disk?"

He shook his head and took a sip of coffee.

She watched him, wondering where in the world he could be hiding the disk—just as the person trying to steal it was. His office, his home, and he himself had all been searched. She was beginning to get really curious about the disk's hiding place, but she didn't want to ask him. That disk was the only security he had at the moment against his company losing a tremendous amount of money. "Did the person do anything to give themselves away?"

"No. Whoever they are, they're being very careful. They're also very smart." He chuckled. "But then I only hire the best."

"You're joking again." She forked a piece of French toast into her mouth.

"They don't have a chance in hell of getting the master disk, Cassidy."

"But we still don't know who it is. It could be any one of the four of them."

"That's right, but I have a plan, and if it works we should know by tonight who it is." He looked at her. "I'd really like you to come to work with me today."

"Why?"

"Just to be there."

"All right," she said, her will to refuse him quickly dissolving, "then I will."

He smiled. "Good. Now eat your breakfast, and then we can take an energy-conserving shower together."

Her lips twisted into a wry smile. "I didn't find our last energy-saving shower very energy saving. In fact I was exhausted by the time—"

"*Cassidy!* You made a joke!"

She set her jaw into a stubborn line. "That wasn't a joke. It was the truth."

"Nothing is funnier than the truth."

She sighed. "Another 'Zachism.'"

"What was that sigh? Resignation? Acceptance? Surrender?"

She wasn't certain herself, so she chose another subject to talk about. "Marsha told me that you've never brought any other women, rather girlfriends, to work with you before."

"That's right." He set his coffee cup on the nightstand beside him, then placed his tray on the floor by the bed.

She waited until he had straightened and was looking at her again. "But you told me that you did, all the time."

His gaze on her was considering. "I didn't want to scare you away, Cassidy. I wanted you to keep working on the story, to give us more time together. I wanted a chance with you."

"But why? We'd only known each other a short time by then." She was unsure what she was fishing for and equally unsure what she wanted him to say in return, but her heart was pounding like a drum.

"For someone so bright, Cassidy, you can be really slow." He rolled to his side, propped himself up on his elbows, and gazed straight into her eyes. "I love you."

Fear slammed into her, followed immediately by a racing excitement. "Love?"

He smiled tenderly. "Don't take it so hard, sweetheart. I'm not going to ask anything of you, at least nothing more than you're willing to give. I'm a very patient man. Sooner or later I'm going to get what I want."

"And what is that?" she asked, still stunned.

"You, of course. You're going to realize you love me too."

She didn't know what to think. She hardly knew what to say. She had always regarded man—woman love as something that she had no use for. In her view, romantic love was a fairy tale with no substance, a myth with no reality. But here he was, saying he loved her.

"Zach, I don't want to hurt you, but I was very

up-front with you about not wanting a relation-ship."

"Yes, you were. But look what we have now."

She forced oxygen into her lungs. "A relation-ship."

"By anyone's standards, I'd say we definitely do."

Her tone turned uncertain. "But it's all going to end when the story's done."

"Who made that rule? You'll have your story by tomorrow, Cassidy. But tomorrow night, I ex-pect you to be here with me."

She felt dizzy, elated, scared. "Zach, you're going to have to give me time."

"I'll give you all the time you need, sweetheart, just as long as you'll stay with me."

Nine

Much to Cassidy's relief, Zach dropped the subject of love. In fact, for a while, he stopped talking altogether. Instead, he took her with him into the shower. And as they both had known would happen, the small space of the shower, combined with their slick, naked bodies, the scented soap, and the warm water, proved too much of a temptation. They made love until they could barely stay upright.

Later, while they were dressing, he explained his plan to her, and she couldn't help but approve. He had been right when he said she would have her story by the next day. It would be a good story and give her a higher profile at the paper. But would she really stay with him once she had it?

They drove separate cars to work, but once there, they spent the day together. Zach insisted that she go on the rounds of the plant with him again. She went and had a wonderful time. She enjoyed watching the way he interacted with his employees in such an easy, genuine way. And she was left light-headed by the speed with which he applied his intellect to problems and came up with solutions.

She had come to terms with the love he had for his company and the toys it produced, but she was still trying to come to terms with his love of her. She was very aware, however, that she was fighting herself, not him.

Once during the day when Zach had stepped away from the office, she saw Deep Teddy Bear, as she persisted in thinking of him, and called him into the office.

Delbert was slightly more composed than at their last meeting. "Do you think Mr. Bennett is mad at me?" he asked anxiously.

"No, of course not. If it wasn't for you contacting me, he wouldn't have known to be on the lookout for this theft."

"I hope he's not mad at me. I'd hate to lose my job. I really like it here."

"I don't understand, Delbert. You are the only person I've seen here who is afraid of Zach. Why?"

"Don't get me wrong. I really admire him. He's sort of like my hero. But he's also kind of spooky. Sometimes I think he's got a special hookup to outer space, the way he comes up with these really great ideas. He's smarter than anyone I've ever known, and this whole place rests on his shoulders and his alone. I wouldn't have a job if it weren't for him."

She nodded thoughtfully. "I guess I see what you mean."

Right before quitting time, Zach called a meeting of the supervisors. On his desk were eight three-and-a-half–inch disks, all neatly labeled as being one of the four parts of the video game that they had handed in.

Zach leaned back in his chair, completely relaxed. But Cassidy noted that he wasn't playing, a sign of how deeply disturbed he was.

"The Game is finished and on time," he said. "I want to thank each of you for doing such a splendid job."

Janet smiled. "How could we help but do a splendid job? We just followed your specs, Zach."

"Nevertheless, you and your groups put in a lot of hard work, and you deserve a great deal of thanks."

Will's grin was spread from ear to ear. "I've had a blast, and I've learned a lot."

"We all have," Brad said, crossing one perfectly creased trouser leg over the other.

"Definitely," Mitchell said.

Zach nodded. "Good. I'm counting on this being a runaway hit with the kids."

"I don't see how it can fail," Brad said. "I gather marketing is already gearing up?"

Zach nodded. "That's right. I'll work tonight at home to put your four disks together with my master, then we'll be ready to hit the ground running tomorrow."

"Great," Mitchell said, "I've promised my grandsons one out of the first batch."

Zach grinned. "I think we can arrange that."

Cassidy sat at an angle to Zach and facing Will, Janet, Mitchell, and Brad. Something continued to nag at her, something she couldn't quite put her finger on. It was almost as if she had seen something or heard something during these last few days that could tell her which one of the four was the culprit.

"How hard is it going to be to integrate our four disks with yours?" Will asked curiously.

"Not hard, it'll just take a little time. I'll do it tonight after dinner and work until I'm finished." He turned and smiled at Cassidy. "It's Lily's night off. I guess you'll have to put up with my cooking."

She'd been concentrating so hard on the four supervisors, his sudden attention on her took her by surprise. "Uh, that's fine with me."

Will leaned forward eagerly. "We can't wait to see this master disk of yours, Zach. It may be called the eighth wonder of the world once The Game hits the stores."

Zach chuckled. "It's not a cure for cancer, folks."

Much to her amazement, Cassidy found herself speaking up. "But think of all the hours of pleasure and happiness it will bring the children of the world."

Janet nodded. "She's right. That master disk of yours will make a product that is going to be spectacular, Zach."

Brad burst out laughing. "I don't know how I'm going to sleep tonight. I'll be living to get back here tomorrow so that I can see it."

Mitchell grinned. "You're not going to be alone."

Zach held up his hands. "I'll do my best not to disappoint you. In the meantime, why don't you start tying up the odds and ends for your respective groups, because next Monday, bright and early, I have a new project for you."

Will's eyes widened. "What? What is it?"

Zach smiled at him. "Monday, Will. Until then, relax. You've earned it."

With good-natured bantering, the four supervisors rose and left the office.

Zach turned to Cassidy. "Well?"

She shrugged. "I don't know. I guess we're going to find out soon, though."

"I almost wish we didn't have to." He grimaced. "And I wish this wasn't going to be so hard on you."

He leaned forward and reached to take her hand. "I'll get through it, thanks to you."

A sweetness rushed through her veins, and she felt like she was melting inside. Zach was simply the most irresistible man she had ever met, she thought ruefully. So how was she going to resist him?

A little later, as they were about to leave the building, Marsha rushed up to them. "Cassidy, your office just called and asked that you go over there right away."

She frowned. "Was there a message about what was up?"

Marsha shook her head. "Nothing except that it was important, and you were to come immediately."

"Thanks, Marsha." She looked at Zach. "I'm sorry. I shouldn't be longer than an hour, but if I am, I'll call you."

"All right. I'll wait for you at the house." He drew her into his arms and kissed her. "Hurry."

She nodded. "I will."

•   •   •

The drive to the newspaper didn't take long. She'd parked, and was just shutting the door when a van pulled up beside her. Before she knew what was happening, a man jumped out, yanked a burlap bag down over her head, and shoved her into the van. The van started rolling immediately.

She had been kidnapped in a matter of seconds.

Her heart raced a mile a minute. She tried to sit up, but someone pushed her back down to the cold metal floor. The van was traveling at a high rate of speed. She could hear the road through the floor, feel every bump and vibration. Nausea churned in her stomach and rose in her throat.

She tried again to sit up, but steellike arms thrust her back down.

"Please . . . who are you? Why are you doing this?"

"Shut up," a rough voice said, and lifted the bag only far enough to cram some sort of rag into her mouth, gagging her.

It was hard for her to gauge how long they traveled. She was too busy trying to control her fear and her churning stomach. With the gag in her mouth, she'd strangle to death if she threw up. And her situation didn't get any better once they stopped. Hands jerked her from the van and propelled her along a walkway and through a door. Obviously inside a building now, she thought for a moment she sensed a third person. But then they started her walking at a fast pace. Suddenly they were in a stairwell, plunging down the stairs. She would have fallen except now two pairs of hands held her in a viselike grip.

They continued down, down. They stopped. A door was opened. Hands against her back shoved her forward. The door closed behind her, and locks clicked and snapped into place. The last thing she heard were boxes being shoved in front of the door. Then there was silence.

She didn't try to move. She waited, disoriented and swaying dizzily. When nothing else happened, she tentatively reached for the burlap bag and pulled it off her head. No one stopped her, so she went a step further and pulled the gag from her mouth. At first everything seemed blurry and dim to her. She closed her eyes and opened them again. This time shapes formed and gained definition. She was at the top of a set of wooden stairs that led down to a room of some sort. The room was dark except for a lantern sitting in the middle of it on a crate. Her heart slammed against her ribs with a sickening force.

She whirled back to the door and tried to open it, but it wouldn't budge. She pounded on the door and yelled, but no one answered her. She turned back to the room. Wrapping her arms around herself, she slowly descended the stairs.

Where was she? And why?

The room smelled damp and moldy, like a muddy river. She picked up the lantern and walked in a broad circle. There were a few crates and boxes sitting against the walls, all watermarked. A greenish mold grew on the walls.

"Oh, no," she whispered.

The lantern's flame wavered as she swayed. She lifted the lantern higher, very much afraid she knew what she was about to see.

Water marks.

They circled the four walls inches from the ceiling.

A sob of terror escaped her throat. *Heaven help her.* She was in the subbasement of Bennett Toys, the same subbasement Zach had told her he was going to have sealed up because it flooded every time it rained. He hadn't mentioned when, she remembered. But one thing was sure. If it rained and the room filled with water, she would drown.

And even if it didn't rain, no one was going to find her. She could die in this dark, dank hole in the ground.

Zach frowned as he checked his watch once more. Cassidy had said she would call if she was longer than an hour, and it had already been two hours. He stared broodingly at the phone, trying to envision what might be happening with her. He supposed the paper could have needed her for a breaking story, and once she set to work on it, she had lost track of the time. Or she could have even gone home to change and fallen asleep in the bathtub. On the other hand . . .

He reached for the phone and called the paper. "Cassidy Stuart, please."

"Just a minute." The woman who answered put him on hold, then after a few moments came back on the line. "I'm sorry. She's not here."

Zach's frown deepened. "She was called into work a couple of hours ago. Could you check again, ask around?"

"I'll try." The woman's tone was grudging, but

this time she was gone longer than before. "I'm sorry, sir," she said when she came back on the line, "but no one has seen her this evening. And as far as I could find out, no one called her either."

"Thank you."

Seized by alarm, Zach broke the connection and quickly dialed Cassidy's house. The phone rang and rang. He let it ring ten times before he slammed the receiver into its cradle with an audible curse.

He had expected the person who was after the master disk to try some sort of diversion to draw him away from the house tonight, but it had never once occurred to him that it might involve Cassidy. He cursed again.

The next half hour blurred for Zach. He drove to her house, but it was dark and locked up. Next he raced over to the newspaper. In the parking lot he found her car.

Zach drew a deep breath in an effort to compose himself. He stared at her car. The son of a bitch had kidnapped her.

Nightmares appeared unbidden in his mind. What if he couldn't find her? What if she was scared and in pain somewhere? What if they had killed her?

He clamped his hands onto the steering wheel. *Think. Think.* He had been so certain he was prepared for all contingencies. Until this moment it had been a game to him, but now Cassidy was in danger and this was a deadly serious situation. He had failed to understand the extent of the thief's desperation, and as a result the thief had moved in a direction he hadn't expected. Whoever it was had somehow known that Cassidy was his one blind spot. The thief knew him well. And that meant he knew the thief well.

Up until this moment, he hadn't seriously tried to figure out which of the four supervisors was trying to steal The Game from him, but now he had no choice but to do so.

He sat in the newspaper's parking lot and considered the possibilities.

He was silent for perhaps a minute. Then . . .

"That's who," he said quietly. "Dammit, that's who it is."

The truth was he had probably known all along, but he hadn't wanted to face it. And because he hadn't, the thief was more than likely in his study right now, taking the disk marked "Master." And Cassidy was alone somewhere, afraid and possibly hurt.

He slammed his fist against the steering wheel. He had to find her.

Cassidy held her wrist close to the lantern and checked her watch. It hadn't been that long since they had shoved her into the subbasement, but she felt as if it had been forever. She had tried once again to get the door open by throwing her body against it, but it was solid. To her surprise, besides the lantern and a jug of oil, she had found a blanket, a canteen of water, and a basket with cheese and bread. Somehow it was hard for her to credit the men who had brought her here with providing these comforts.

She was sure they were the same thugs who had attacked Zach.

"Thugs R Us," she said aloud, and smiled, reassured by both the sound of her voice and Zach's joke about the men.

Her gaze went to the high-water mark near the ceiling, and wished she knew if it was supposed to rain. Unfortunately she hadn't seen a weather forecast in days, not since she had begun spending all her time with Zach.

"Zach."

Speaking his name into the dank, moldy air made her feel better. But would he find her? Once he realized something was wrong, she had no doubt he would try. But could he really do it?

With one more glance at the water marks, she took the lantern and set out to explore her windowless surroundings in a deliberate attempt to get her mind off the danger she was in. She also hoped to find something that could be of use to her.

She found boxes of Bennett Blocks shoved way back in the corner beneath the stairs. She pulled the boxes out and opened them one by one. One box held red blocks, another blue, a third yellow.

She dragged the box of red blocks over to the center of the room and dumped them out onto the floor. Then she spread the blanket over the cold concrete, sat down, and began to play.

She would build a castle, she thought, like the one she had worked on with Zach the first night they had made love. It might not make her feel any better, she thought, but if she were lucky, it would help pass the time.

Help pass the time until what? she asked herself, but her mind refused to answer.

But as she chose first one block, then the next for the castle, a strange thing began to happen. Her fears quieted, her nerves calmed. And she began to think.

They had left her a blanket, water, and a basket of cheese and bread, essentials to stay alive when locked in a cold place for any length of time. But they also had left her a lantern and a jug of oil, a nicety, but certainly not a necessity to life. No, the lantern was more something someone would think of who could empathize and understand how frightened she would be in the dark. Either the guys from Thugs R Us were extremely sensitive, caring men . . .

She chose another block and cast her mind back to what she had learned about the four supervisors in the past few days. Janet was competent and dedicated, Will was young and enthusiastic, Mitchell solid and dependable, Brad smart and flashy.

Cassidy went still as she remembered what it was she had heard that had been nagging at her. *That was it.* She knew which of the four was trying to steal the video game. For a moment, she allowed herself to feel a tremendous rush of pride in herself, then reality crept back in. Knowing who the thief was would do her no good as long as she was locked up in this hole in the ground.

She looked down at the block in her hand. She studied its shape and felt its weight and reflected on the man who had created it. Zach, a man with dreams in his eyes and stuffed animals on his bed. A man who had written the specs for this revolutionary new set of blocks on the back of another man's shirt. A man who had said he loved her. A man who had said she could depend on him.

Zach.

She was going to get out, she thought with sudden and complete confidence.

Zach was going to find her. And when he did, she was going to tell him something that unconsciously she had known for a long time but had been too blind to realize.

She was going to tell him she loved him.

Zach broke all speed records getting to Bennett Toys, and he prayed all the way. Once there, he questioned the security people and received the answer he had expected. With the security guards trailing behind him, he ran across the grounds to the one plant that had been built with a subbasement.

By the time the guards had caught up with him, he had plowed through the boxes hiding the subbasement's door and its obviously new padlock. One of the guards had had the foresight to bring a tire iron with him. A great portent of his future with Bennett Toys, Zach thought. In moments he had broken the padlock and wrested open the door.

"Cassidy!"

As she looked up the stairs, her body shuddered violently and her eyes filled with tears. "Oh, Zach"—a sob of emotion choked her words—"I knew you'd find me."

He bounded down the stairs; she started toward him. They met, he pulled her into his arms, and she went, burying her face in his chest, drawing in deep breaths of him.

"Lord, I was so scared, Cassidy. I was so afraid I wouldn't find you." He hugged her to him. Her skin felt cold, but she was alive, and her body molded to his as if she had never been apart from him. Feeling her heart beat against his, he seriously wondered if he would ever be able to let her go, but soon the urgency to see her lovely face got the better of him. He drew back and saw the scratch on her cheek she had sustained when they had pushed her to the floor of the van. "What did they do to you? Are you all right? Did they hurt you? If they so much as laid a finger on you—"

Laughter bubbled up from her heart and filled the air around them. "I'm fine. Oh, Zach, I knew you would come for me. I love you so much."

He made a sound of disbelief. "Would you mind repeating that?"

"I love you, Zach."

In the light from the lamp's flame, his face showed shadows of a new vulnerability. "Cassidy, you've just had a bad scare, and now I've come to your rescue. It's understandable—"

She reached up and framed his face with her hands. "I love you, Zach."

"Is it really true?" he whispered huskily.

She nodded, her eyes filling with tears. "Yes, it's really true."

Unmindful of the security guards who were waiting discreetly at the top of the stairs, he bent his head and kissed her until her tears were dried and her body was warmed. "I love you more than I can even begin to tell you," he said. "Come on. I'm taking you home."

"No, wait. Look at the castle I built."

His eyebrows arched in surprise. "There were blocks down here?"

"Yes, and thank heavens there were. They helped me."

He didn't have to ask her to explain what she meant. The enchanting red block fortress said it all. He smiled. "It's wonderful. I'll make arrangements to have it brought up intact."

She shook her head, her eyes gleaming with happiness. "No, leave it here. We'll make lots of other castles together."

They didn't talk much that night. Instead, in Zach's bed, they let the actions of their bodies express their feelings. They spoke of love and of passion and of their ecstasy.

And when at last they tired, Zach drew her back against him and curled around her spoon-fashion.

"Zach?" Cassidy murmured, right before she fell asleep.

"Ummm?"

"They didn't get the master disk, did they?"

"No."

"I didn't think so. I know where the master disk is."

And in the dark he smiled, because he realized she had finally figured him out.

Ten

Sitting in Zach's office the next morning, Cassidy held the baby doll in her lap, taking comfort in the doll's cuddly little body and soft warmth. She didn't relish what was about to happen, though her story would most assuredly make the front page of the newspaper. She glanced at Zach, but he seemed to be feeling none of the nervousness she was experiencing as he leaned back in his big chair and watched Will, Janet, Mitchell, and Brad file into his office and take seats.

Will rubbed his hands together with excitement. "Well? Where is it?"

"Yeah," Brad said with a big grin. "When can we see it? Do you have it here?"

"Did it turn out as wonderful as we all expected?" Janet asked brightly.

Mitchell chuckled. "Come on, Zach. Don't keep us in suspense. Where is it?"

Zach held up his hand. "You'll get to see it in

due time, I promise. But first there's something I have to tell you."

Will's excitement faded to a visible anxiousness. "What is it? Everything's all right, isn't it?"

Zach nodded. "Yes. Thanks to Cassidy. You see, several days ago she received a tip that someone in our company was about to steal The Game and sell it to a foreign competitor for ten million dollars."

Brad almost came out of his chair. "*What?*"

Mitchell's eyebrows disappeared up into his hairline. "Someone who *works* for you, Zach?"

"That's right. And whoever it is would have had to copy the four disks and then the master."

"But how could that happen?" Will asked, sitting forward. "We turned the disks into you at the end of every day, and you always had the master."

Zach's gaze rested on each of them in turn. "Nevertheless, this person managed to copy the four disks during working hours, and then went after the master. Both my office and home were searched, and I was mugged."

"Good Lord!" Mitchell said explosively.

"That's not all. Last night the person did even worse. After I announced that I would be working at home, assembling The Game, this person arranged to have Cassidy kidnapped so that I would be drawn away from the house to look for her."

Four pairs of eyes went to Cassidy.

"Are you okay?" Will asked her.

"Were you hurt?" Janet asked.

She hugged the baby doll to her. "No. Thanks to Zach, I'm fine. He figured out where they had taken me."

"Wait a minute," Brad said, his voice quiet. "You said after you announced you would be working at home. You announced that to the four of us."

Zach nodded. "That's right."

"You mean you suspect one of us?" Mitchell asked, his tone incredulous.

"Think about it," Zach said gently. "It has to be one of you. You're the only ones who could possibly manage to copy all four disks."

Will slammed his fist into the opposite palm. "Damn."

Zach sent a red Hot Wheels Volkswagen rolling across his desk. It stopped by itself about an inch from the edge. "I'm sorry to have to tell you, but it's true. I didn't know exactly who it was, though, until last night. Figuring out who did it helped me determine where Cassidy was."

Will looked astounded. "You mean you know who this person is?" He glanced at the other three.

Janet spoke up. "But is it speculation on your part, or do you actually have proof? Since it involves one of us, I think we deserve to know."

"If you'd been in the car with me last night when I realized who it was, I'm sure you would have called it speculation. And even though I was pretty sure I was right, I couldn't be a hundred percent certain Cassidy was where I thought she was until I actually went there and found her."

"But is finding Cassidy proof of the person's guilt?" Brad asked with a frown.

Zach shook his head. "No, this is." He opened a drawer, withdrew a videotape, and threw it onto his desk. "I had a camera set up in my study at home last night to record who came to get the disk. The attempted theft and the thief were captured in living color on the tape."

Stunned silence filled the room. From her vantage point facing them, Cassidy could tell that three of the supervisors were so shocked they didn't know what to think. But the blood had drained from the real culprit's face.

"You said *attempted* theft," Will said, his voice shaking now. "Does that mean the master disk is still safe?"

Zach nodded. "The person took a disk from my computer marked "Master," but it was completely blank." He paused for a moment, then looked straight at Janet. "Wasn't it?"

"Good Lord," Mitchell murmured in shock.

Brad sadly shook his head and looked away.

Will stared at her in amazement.

"Gentlemen," Zach said, still holding Janet's gaze, "would you mind leaving us alone, please? I'll fill you in on everything later."

With difficulty Brad cleared his throat. "Sure Zach."

"No problem," Will said.

With awkward glances at Janet, the three men left the room. Mitchell was the last out, and he shut the door behind him.

Zach glanced at Cassidy. He could only guess at how hard she was finding it to face the person who had put her through so much. "You don't have to stay."

"I know," she said, "but I want to. I want to know *why*."

"That's what Janet is about to tell us." He looked back at her. She was sitting stiff as a board; only her chest moved, rising and falling at an abnormally fast pace. "Janet? It wasn't only greed, was it?"

Her cheeks flared red in a face otherwise devoid of color. "You bastard! Everything is so damned easy for you."

He flicked another glance at Cassidy, reassuring himself that she really was all right. "Not everything. It took me quite a while to figure out where you had those two thugs take Cassidy last night. But once I realized it was you, it became easier."

"How?" she asked, her voice brittle. "I thought the subbasement would be the last place anyone would think of."

"To start with, places to hide a person are not that easy to come by. You'd need someplace secure, where someone could be constrained and not heard. There weren't too many places like that I could think of. But I had something going for me. My knowledge of you. You always go with the familiar, Janet. That narrowed the field to your condo and here, and the area around your condo is too populated—"

"What do you mean, I always go with the familiar?"

"I've seen it in your work time and again."

"Am I that bad?"

"If you were, I wouldn't have kept you on."

She seemed to slump, though she didn't actually move. "For five years I've watched you." She shook her head in amazement, as if she still couldn't believe what she had seen and learned. "When I first came to work for you five years ago, I had my eyes set on the stars. I thought I would be able to write brilliant programs and create wondrous, marvelous things. Then gradually as the months and years passed and I watched and worked with you, I began to realize what true brilliance was." She blinked away angry tears. "Time and again I've seen you spin an idea out of thin air and create something from nothing that absolutely took my breath away and everybody else's. And I came to understand that much as I wanted to, I'd never be able to take people's breath away with something I created."

His expression solemn, Zach steepled his fingers together. "And so you came to resent me."

Janet gave a short laugh that was full of pain. "It's funny. I was half in love with you when I first started working for you, but you never saw me as a woman."

"I saw you as a more-than-capable computer expert, Janet, and a valued colleague. But apparently that wasn't enough for you."

Janet looked down at her hands; she had twisted them together in her lap. "No, that wasn't enough. I decided I'd get the money while I could and get out of the business."

"Yet you came to work today."

"I didn't know that you knew the master disk was in jeopardy. And I sure as hell didn't know about the damned camera. I thought that even though I had lost the sale, I could arrange for Cassidy to be released without anyone figuring out who or why, and still hold onto my job."

"Until you found something else to steal?"

"That's exactly right," she said, tortured and arrogant. "I was going to use you by continuing to take your money until I could find something else to take away from you."

Zach rubbed his eyes with a thumb and finger, chasing a phantom ache. "The police are waiting for you in the lobby, Janet."

Fear rushed into her eyes and claimed her expression.

"I'm sorry," he said, his jaw taut. "I truly am. I would have been inclined to fire you and let it go at that, figuring that the loss of your job and the money would have been enough punishment. But you made the mistake of bringing Cassidy into it. You went one step too far, Janet."

She rose unsteadily to her feet. "I know, but I knew that snatching her was the only way I could get you out of the house. If it had started to rain, I would have seen to it that she got out."

"Thank you for the lantern," Cassidy said, feeling a debt of gratitude toward the woman even though it was her fault she had needed it.

A grim smile touched Janet's lips. "If it had been me down there, I would have been terrified without a light." She started for the door, then turned back. "I've got to know, Zach. You've got to tell me. Where is the master disk?"

He lifted a forefinger to his head and tapped his temple. "It's here. It's always been here."

Janet's laugh carried a thread of hysteria, and watching, Cassidy understood. It hadn't been a piece of technology that had defeated Janet, but rather a piece of brilliant creativity, the very thing that made Zach the out-of-the-ordinary creator he was, and the very thing that Janet would never have.

"Janet," Zach said. "Tell the police about the thugs you hired, and they may go easier on you." His gaze stayed on the proud line of her back as she left the room. When the door closed behind her, he expelled a long stream of breath and let his head fall back against his chair's headrest.

Cassidy set aside the baby doll and reached to cover Zach's hand with hers. "Don't take it so hard. You're not responsible for what she did."

He rolled his head from side to side along the chair's back as if he still couldn't believe it. "I liked and respected Janet. But by putting you in danger, she forced me to face the fact that it was she who was trying to steal from me."

"How did you come to realize it was Janet?"

He shrugged. "I'm not even sure. It was just a very certain feeling, like something I had really known all along. And then I came here and the security guards confirmed that she was the only one who had left the building late. She had probably made it a point to learn the security routine when she was looking for the master disk. I'm sure she had the kidnapping plan set to go, waiting for when I announced I would be working on the master disk, and where. Then when the time came, she stayed behind to slip you and her cohorts into the plant between security rounds and direct them to the subbasement. When I think of what she put you through—"

Her hand tightened over his. "It's all right. I built the castle, and I thought. It was how I remembered what had been nagging at me. She had said she was the only one of them who hadn't missed a day of work with that cold they'd all had. She must have copied their disks on the days they were out sick."

Zach stared at her for a long moment. "Thank you."

"For what?"

"For wearing red to the party."

She smiled. "I'll tell you something I haven't told you before. Red's my favorite color too."

His lips curved upward, but his expression remained serious. "And thank you for confiding in me about the theft."

She made a face. "I'd like to meet the person who could hold out information from you, because I sure couldn't."

"And thank you for loving me."

She went soft inside. "I do. I only *thought* I had a chance at resisting you. But the reality was, you bowled me over right from the start."

A faint twinkle danced into his eyes. "Let's go home and play."

"What a good idea."

"Tell me the truth," Cassidy said, addressing Zach across the train tracks in his study. "The stuffed animals are reproducing, aren't they?"

Zach smiled at her. She was wearing a red jump suit and sitting cross-legged on the floor across from him. "What makes you say that?"

"I see at least ten new stuffed animals in here. This zebra for instance." She pointed to the black and white animal lying against her knee. "I'm sure I've never seen him before. And what about this ostrich?" The fluffy bird's long neck was across her ankle. "And then there's this guy." She picked up the cushy and amiable buffalo that had been resting comfortably against her thigh.

Lily glanced over at her from her position beside Bobby. They were at Zach's computer, playing with the just-put-together prototype of The Game. "I hate to tell you, sugar, but this house is a veritable stuffed animal jungle."

"If they bother you, I guess we could confine them to one area of the house," Zach said.

"No, don't be silly. They're actually sort of sweet, the way they seem to cluster around me no matter where I am."

"Children," Lily said unexpectedly. "I understand children are sweet too."

"Yeah, but you have to feed them," Bobby said, surprising everyone by following the conversation, even though his eyes were glued to the computer screen.

"What's so hard?" Lily asked. "You stick the food in their mouths, and they eat it."

Cassidy's lips twitched, wondering how the conversation had gotten away from her. "Have you ever heard of good, old-fashioned, basic teddy bears, Zach? I mean whoever heard of a stuffed ostrich?"

Leaning down so that his head touched the carpet, he critically eyed the wheel alignment of a boxcar. "We have teddy bears. I'm sure we do. Lily, where are the teddy bears?"

"There's nothing more basic and old-fashioned than children," she mumbled in answer. "Children, yes sirree."

Cassidy caught Zach's eyes as he straightened, and whispered to him, "Does Lily have something in particular on her mind?"

He chuckled, and whispered back, "Lily doesn't believe in keeping anything on her mind. She has a philosophy about sharing."

"Cassidy was born to be a mother," Bobby said abruptly. "Look how well I turned out." He immediately returned his attention to The Game. "This is awesome, Zach."

"Thanks."

Cassidy cleared his throat. "I thought we were talking about stuffed animals."

"After I finish my ikebana class, I'm thinking about signing up for a nanny class," Lily said loudly to no one in particular.

Cassidy colored in embarrassment at Lily's, and even Bobby's, comments. She hoped that Zach wasn't equally embarrassed. In a relatively short time she had fallen deeply in love with him. But she didn't believe in moving too fast. They had plenty of time. . . .

She looked over at him, and he winked.

Her heart somersaulted with tenderness and love. She was well and truly lost, she thought, if such a simple gesture could make her feel so good.

He took a rolled-up piece of paper from his pocket and put it in the open boxcar in front of him. Then he started the train. It made its circles and loops around the little town, up the sofa cushion, around a bowl of water that apparently represented a lake. Finally it stopped in front of her.

She automatically reached for the tiny silver coal scoop, but then she noticed the rolled-up piece of paper.

She glanced at him and saw an expectant expression on his face. She looked over at Lily and Bobby and saw the same expressions on their faces. "What—"

"It's for you," Zach said.

She took the piece of paper from the boxcar and unrolled it. A large, dazzling diamond solitaire tumbled into her lap. "Good heavens, Zach. What is this?"

"Your basic, old-fashioned engagement ring. It was my grandmother's"

"Your—" Shock cut off her words. She looked down at the paper. It read, "Will you marry me?"

"Well?" he said softly. "Will you marry me, Cassidy?"

Pure unadulterated joy flooded through her with such a rush that her eyes filled with tears and emotion clogged her throat.

"Yes, she will," Bobby said, abandoning The Game with glee.

"Of course she will," Lily said emphatically.

"Well?" Zach asked, his blue eyes twinkling more than she had ever seen them.

"Yes," she said happily, forgetting forever her thoughts about not moving too fast. "I will."

Bobby and Lily cheered and hugged each other.

Zach surged to his feet, stepped over the

tracks and the little town, and pulled her up into his arms. "I love you, Cassidy."

She blinked away her tears. "And I love you."

He drew away from her only long enough to slip the ring onto her finger.

Over at the desk, Lily and Bobby fell into a discussion about which room would be his.

The stuffed toys regrouped themselves around Cassidy's legs.

And Zach bent his head and kissed her, putting a seal on their future together, a future they both knew would be bursting with love, happiness, toys, stuffed animals, and lots of happy, healthy, giggling children.

THE EDITOR'S CORNER

LOVESWEPT sails into autumn with six marvelous romances featuring passionate, independent, and truly remarkable heroines. And you can be sure they each find the wonderful heroes they deserve. With temperatures starting to drop and daylight hours becoming shorter, there's no better time to cuddle up with a LOVESWEPT!

Leading our lineup for October is **IN ANNIE'S EYES** by Billie Green, LOVESWEPT #504. This emotionally powerful story is an example of the author's great skill in touching our hearts. Max Decatur was her first lover and her only love, and marrying him was Anne Seaton's dream come true. But in a moment of confusion and sorrow she left him, believing she stood in the way of his promising career. Now after eleven lonely years he's back in her life, and she's ready to face his anger and furious revenge. Max waited forever to hurt her, but seeing her again ignites long-buried desire. And suddenly nothing matters but rekindling the old flame of passion. . . . An absolute winner!

Linda Cajio comes up with the most unlikely couple—and plenty of laughter—in the utterly enchanting **NIGHT MUSIC**, LOVESWEPT #505. Hilary Rayburn can't turn down Devlin Kitteridge's scheme to bring her grandfather and his matchmaking grandmother together more than sixty years after a broken engagement—even if it means carrying on a charade as lovers. Dev and Hilary have nothing in common but their plan, yet she can't catch her breath when he draws her close and kisses her into sweet oblivion. Dev wants no part of this elegant social butterfly—until he succumbs to her sizzling warmth and vulnerable softness. You'll be thoroughly entertained as these two couples find their way to happy-ever-after.

Many of you might think of that wonderful song "Some Enchanted Evening" when you read the opening scenes of **TO GIVE A HEART WINGS** by Mary Kay McComas, LOVESWEPT #506. For it is across a crowded room that Colt McKinnon first spots Hannah Alexander, and right away he knows he must claim her. When he takes her hand to dance and feels her body cleave to his with electric satisfaction, this daredevil racer finally believes in love at first sight. But when the music stops Hannah escapes before he can discover her secret pain. How is she to know that he would track her down, determined to possess her and slay her dragons? There's no resisting Colt's strong arms and tender smile, and finally Hannah discovers how wonderful it is to fly on the wings of love.

A vacation in the Caribbean turns into an exciting and passionate adventure in **DATE WITH THE DEVIL** by Olivia Rupprecht, LOVESWEPT #507. When prim and proper Diedre Forsythe is marooned on an island in the Bermuda Triangle with only martial arts master Sterling Jakes for a companion, she thinks she's in trouble. She doesn't expect the thrill of Sterling's survival training or his spellbinding seduction. Finally she throws caution to the wind and surrenders to the risky promise of his intimate caress. He's a man of secrets and shadows, but he's also her destiny, her soulmate. If they're ever rescued from their paradise, would her newfound courage be strong enough to hold him? This is a riveting story written with great sensuality.

The latest from Lori Copeland, **MELANCHOLY BABY,** LOVE-SWEPT #508, will have you sighing for its handsome hell-raiser of a hero. Bud Huntington was the best-looking boy in high school, and the wildest—but now the reckless rebel is the local doctor, and the most gorgeous man Teal Anderson has seen. She wants him as much as ever—and Bud knows it! He understands just how to tease the cool redhead, to stoke the flames of her long-suppressed desire with kisses that demand a lifetime commitment. Teal shook off the dust of her small Missouri hometown for the excitement of a big city years ago, but circumstances forced her to return, and now in Bud's arms she knows she'll never be a melancholy baby again. You'll be enthralled with the way these two confront and solve their problems.

There can't be a more appropriate title than **DANGEROUS PROPOSITION** for Judy Gill's next LOVESWEPT, #509. It's bad enough that widow Liss Tremayne has to drive through a blizzard to get to the cattle ranch she's recently inherited, but she knows when she gets there she'll be sharing the place with a man who doesn't want her around. Still, Liss will dare anything to provide a good life for her two young sons. Kirk Allbright has his own reasons for wishing Liss hasn't invaded his sanctuary: the feminine scent of her hair, the silky feel of her skin, the sensual glow in her dark eyes—all are perilous to a cowboy who finds it hard to trust anyone. But the cold ache in their hearts melts as warm winter nights begin to work their magic. . . . You'll relish every moment in this touching love story.

FANFARE presents four truly spectacular books next month! Don't miss out on **RENDEZVOUS,** the new and fabulous historical novel by bestselling author Amanda Quick: **MIRACLE**, an unforgettable contemporary story of love and the collision of two worlds, from critically acclaimed Deborah Smith: **CIRCLE OF PEARLS**, a thrilling historical by immensely talented Rosalind Laker; and **FOREVER**, by Theresa Weir, a heart-grabbing contemporary romance.

Happy reading!

With warmest wishes,

Nita Taublib

Nita Taublib
Associate Publisher/LOVESWEPT
Publishing Associate/FANFARE

FANFARE SPECIAL OFFER

Be one of the first 100 people to collect 6 FANFARE logos (marked "special offer") and send them in with the completed coupon below. We'll send the first 50 people an autographed copy of Fayrene Preston's THE SWANSEA DESTINY, on sale in September! The second 50 people will receive an autographed copy of Deborah Smith's MIRACLE, on sale in October!

The FANFARE logos you need to collect are in the back of LOVESWEPT books #498 through #503. There is one FANFARE logo in the back of each book.

For a chance to receive an autographed copy of THE SWANSEA DESTINY or MIRACLE, fill in the coupon below (no photocopies or facsimiles allowed), cut it out and send it along with the 6 logos to:

FANFARE Special Offer
Department CK
Bantam Books
666 Fifth Avenue
New York, New York 10103

- - - - - - - - - - - - - - - - - - -

Here's my coupon and my 6 logos! If I am one of the first 50 people whose coupon you receive, please send me an autographed copy of THE SWANSEA DESTINY. If I am one of the second 50 people whose coupon you receive, please send me an autographed copy of MIRACLE.

Name _____

Address _____

City/State/Zip _____

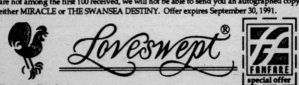

Loveswept ®

FANFARE
special offer

Bantam Books   SW 9 - 10/91   cut on dotted line

THE LATEST IN BOOKS AND AUDIO CASSETTES

Paperbacks

☐	28671	**NOBODY'S FAULT** Nancy Holmes	$5.95
☐	28412	**A SEASON OF SWANS** Celeste De Blasis	$5.95
☐	28354	**SEDUCTION** Amanda Quick	$4.50
☐	28594	**SURRENDER** Amanda Quick	$4.50
☐	28435	**WORLD OF DIFFERENCE** Leonia Blair	$5.95
☐	28416	**RIGHTFULLY MINE** Doris Mortman	$5.95
☐	27032	**FIRST BORN** Doris Mortman	$4.95
☐	27283	**BRAZEN VIRTUE** Nora Roberts	$4.50
☐	27891	**PEOPLE LIKE US** Dominick Dunne	$4.95
☐	27260	**WILD SWAN** Celeste De Blasis	$5.95
☐	25692	**SWAN'S CHANCE** Celeste De Blasis	$5.95
☐	27790	**A WOMAN OF SUBSTANCE** Barbara Taylor Bradford	$5.95

Audio

☐	**SEPTEMBER** by Rosamunde Pilcher Performance by Lynn Redgrave 180 Mins. Double Cassette	45241-X	$15.95
☐	**THE SHELL SEEKERS** by Rosamunde Pilcher Performance by Lynn Redgrave 180 Mins. Double Cassette	48183-9	$14.95
☐	**COLD SASSY TREE** by Olive Ann Burns Performance by Richard Thomas 180 Mins. Double Cassette	45166-9	$14.95
☐	**NOBODY'S FAULT** by Nancy Holmes Performance by Geraldine James 180 Mins. Double Cassette	45250-9	$14.95

Bantam Books, Dept. FBS, 414 East Golf Road, Des Plaines, IL 60016

Please send me the items I have checked above. I am enclosing $_____
(please add $2.50 to cover postage and handling). Send check or money order,
no cash or C.O.D.s please. (Tape offer good in USA only.)

Mr/Ms _____

Address _____

City/State _____ Zip _____

FBS–1/91

Please allow four to six weeks for delivery.
Prices and availability subject to change without notice.